"So, are the dorms far from here, Stephanie?" Mark asked as he nibbled his way down her neck.

Stephanie giggled, but as her eyes landed on a gap on the bottom shelf of books, she immediately stiffened. Through the gap that led to the next aisle, she could see a familiar pair of brown shoes.

"What's wrong?" Mark mumbled.

Stephanie didn't answer. The shoes were brown, polished wing tips with skinny little laces. They belonged to Jonathan Baur, Stephanie's boyfriend.

"Hey, Steph—" Mark started to say.

But Stephanie clamped Mark's mouth shut with her perfectly manicured fingers. Then she whisked her hand away and planted a long kiss on his lips, her eyes still glued to the pair of shoes.

NANCY DREW ON CAMPUS™

Available from ARCHWAY Paperbacks

Nancy Drew on Campus™ #21

Love
and Betrayal

Carolyn Keene

AN ARCHWAY PAPERBACK
Published by POCKET BOOKS
New York London Toronto Sydney Tokyo Singapore

AN ARCHWAY PAPERBACK *Original*

An Archway Paperback published by
POCKET BOOKS, a division of Simon & Schuster Inc.
1230 Avenue of the Americas, New York, NY 10020

ISBN: 0-671-00213-9

First Archway Paperback printing May 1997

10 9 8 7 6 5 4 3 2 1

Cover photos by Pat Hill Studio

Printed in the U.S.A.

IL 8+

CHAPTER 1

Nancy Drew was running away.

She had no idea where she was going. All she knew was that she had just seen something terrible. Something that had split her heart wide open.

Ned . . . and Bess?

Nancy could feel the wet grass of the Wilder University campus lawn soaking into her shoes. Sweat trickled down the side of her face, but she couldn't stop—not even for a moment. Her legs kept moving as she desperately tried to get far, far away.

Why didn't it occur to me earlier? Nancy thought wildly. After all, her best friend and old boyfriend had known each other for years. Nancy had dated Ned Nickerson since high school. And she'd hung around with Bess Marvin since they had been little.

Ned was alone now. And since Bess's boy-

friend, Paul Cody, died in a tragic accident, Bess
was alone, too. Suddenly the two of them together made perfect, horrible sense.

Nancy didn't slow down until she neared the
campus lake. Behind her the lights of the dorms
glimmered, but all she could see was the image
of Ned and Bess—together in Bess's room.

She wanted to kick herself. Why hadn't she
knocked on the door before bursting in?

But she and Bess had never knocked before
entering each other's rooms. They'd never had
secrets.

Nancy pushed her long reddish blond hair out
of her face, then wiped her wet cheeks with the
palms of her hands. She tried to reason with herself. Ned and Bess, after all, had only been hugging. And Bess had said several times that Ned
was the only person who seemed to understand
what she was going through after Paul died. They
had definitely gotten to be closer friends over the
last few months.

Another voice inside Nancy insisted that the
two of them had been way too close for a friendly
hug. And if it had been just a friendly hug, why
had Ned acted so shocked, almost horrified, when
he saw her standing in the doorway.

There was also the undeniable fact that Ned
had come to Wilder two days earlier, and never
once had tried to contact Nancy—even to say
hello. It had to be true—her best friend and her
old boyfriend were a couple.

She stared into the dark waters of the lake,

wondering how someone with her sharp instincts could have missed something so completely obvious. Grief and loneliness rippled through her. She'd thought she was completely over Ned Nickerson, but now . . .

"Oh my gosh," she said out loud. "Maybe I'm still in love with him."

"She saw us, Ned," Bess said worriedly. She ducked her head out of her dorm room and scanned the hall for Nancy.

"It's no big deal," Ned said. He stood up and stuffed his sweatshirt into his backpack and zipped it shut. "Nancy knows we're just good friends."

Bess shook her head firmly. "I saw the look on her face, Ned. If she thought it was a hug between friends, why did she take off like that?"

"Nancy's the one who broke up with *me* at the beginning of the semester, Bess," he pointed out.

"Yes, but . . ."

"She took off because she's avoiding me," Ned went on. "Come on. She didn't know my car broke down yesterday. She probably thought I was back at Emerson by now. Then she freaked out when she saw I was still here."

Bess watched him rake back a strand of thick dark hair that had fallen over his eyes. Maybe Ned was right. Maybe that was exactly why Nancy had taken off.

"Besides, Nancy's the one with the new boyfriend," Ned added firmly.

"She doesn't have a new boyfriend anymore. She broke up with Jake Collins, remember?" Bess reminded him.

"I'm still ancient history, Bess," Ned insisted. "There's no way Nancy was upset about the two of us hugging.

"Come on," he added, reaching into the pocket of his leather coat for his keys. "Walk me out to my car."

"Okay." Bess locked her door and followed him down Jamison Hall's brick steps and out to the parking lot. She leaned against Ned's car as he opened the trunk and threw in his pack.

"You really think she wasn't upset?" Bess asked, twirling a long strand of blond hair around her finger.

"Yup." Ned stood in front of her, looking directly into her big blue eyes. "Even if there had been more behind that hug," he said softly, "Nancy knows she doesn't have the right to be angry."

Bess nodded. To her surprise, a blush swept across her face. Suddenly all she could think about was the way it had felt to be spinning in Ned's arms on the dance floor at Club Z the past weekend. There *was* something more to their friendship—at least there had been the other night. In fact, their feelings for each other had been so strong, they'd even talked about them later.

Still, neither one of them could take their relationship to the next level. Bess knew a romance—any romance—right now would end in disaster. It was just too soon after Paul's death. And she wasn't willing to jeopardize her friendship with Ned—or with Nancy.

"Come on, Bess," Ned argued, stuffing his hands into his jeans pockets. "Nancy doesn't want to see me anymore."

Actually, Bess thought guiltily, she herself was responsible for part of that. After Nancy's breakup with Jake, she'd urged Nancy not to fall back on Ned for emotional support. Bess convinced her that it had already been too hard on him.

"Don't worry, Bess, okay?" Ned said. "Nancy's cool—I'm sure about that." Then he cleared his throat. "I'd better go. I've got a long drive and I want to get back to Emerson by midnight."

Before Bess could say anything, she felt Ned lean closer. His shirt brushed her cheek. "Thanks for everything, Ned," she said, hugging him. "It meant a lot to me that you came."

"It was good to see you, Bess," Ned replied. A second later he pulled away from her and climbed into his car.

Bess stood in the darkness, watching as Ned's car moved slowly out of the parking lot. "Ancient history, huh?" she whispered.

If things were so dead between Nancy and Ned, then why did she keep getting the feeling that she was in the way?

* * *

There was one thing Stephanie Keats liked in a man, besides striking good looks.

Actually, there are three things, she thought lazily as she wrapped her arms around Mark Hanson's neck and gave him another long delicious kiss behind the English lit stacks in the Rock, the university library. Broad shoulders. A nice smile. And great clothes.

"Mmmmm," Mark murmured, running both hands through her black hair. He was a tall languid guy with expressive brown eyes and dark hair pulled back in a ponytail. "Where did you say you lived?"

Stephanie sighed. It was true she barely knew Mark. In fact, she'd met him only a half hour ago when she was searching for a discreet corner on the third floor to smoke a cigarette.

Mark had been poring over a large volume of poetry when she boldly walked up and looked over his shoulder. "I love English poetry," Stephanie had told him.

"Oh, really?" Mark had replied with a grin. Things had moved quickly after that.

"So, are the dorms far from here, Stephanie?" Mark asked as he nibbled his way down her neck.

Stephanie giggled and bent her neck farther forward. But as her eyes landed on a gap on the bottom shelf of books, she immediately stiffened. Through the gap that led to the next aisle, she could see a familiar pair of brown shoes.

"What's wrong?" Mark mumbled.

Stephanie didn't answer. They were brown

shoes, polished wing tips, with skinny little laces. They belonged to Jonathan Baur, Stephanie's boyfriend.

"Hey, Steph—" Mark started to say.

But Stephanie clamped Mark's mouth shut with her perfectly manicured fingers. Then she whisked her hand away and planted a long kiss on his lips, her eyes still glued to the pair of shoes.

"But I don't . . ." Mark pulled away.

Panicked, Stephanie grabbed him again for another kiss. Jonathan was at the library because she had told him to meet her there when he got off work. How could she have forgotten?

Continuing to kiss Mark, Stephanie slid a final look down at the gap in the bookcase. To her huge relief, the shoes were gone.

"Stephanie?" Mark said, an eager expression in his dark eyes. "I've got an idea. Let's go back to my place and . . ."

Stephanie wasn't paying attention any longer. Instead, she was focused on the fact that she wanted to kick herself for forgetting that she'd asked Jonathan to meet her after his shift at Berrigan's Department Store was over. Unlike Stephanie's other friends, Jonathan had already graduated from college, and he was now a floor manager at the popular store, where she herself worked part-time at the cosmetics counter.

Plus, Jonathan wasn't just any guy. For the past few weeks they'd been dating each other exclusively. The silver friendship ring he'd given her felt red-hot on her right ring finger. He'd told her he loved her. And every time she thought of his tall strong frame and chestnut hair, she remembered that she loved him, too.

"So what am I doing?" Stephanie muttered.

"What?" Mark said in obvious confusion. "What's up, Stephanie?"

Abruptly she whirled around. "I've gotta go," she dismissed him, marching away down the stacks toward her books. "I need to figure out what I'm doing with my life, and you're not helping."

Stephanie took a deep breath. All she needed to do now was grab a tissue, straighten her lipstick, and find Jonathan before he left the library. Still, there was a heavy feeling in her chest. She was supposed to be in love with Jonathan. And here she was, picking up some guy in the library.

"What kind of person are you?" she said out loud. "Some kind of freak?"

"I love these old black-and-white films," George Fayne said. She curled up her long runner's legs and watched as the opening credits of *A Tale of Two Cities* rolled across the TV screen. After her last class, she'd brought the video over to her boyfriend Will Blackfeather's off-campus apartment so that she could watch it there. Will was sitting next to her, but he wasn't watching the movie.

"Mmmm, I suppose," Will murmured, running a hand down George's leg.

George shifted on the couch, tucking her legs farther under her body. "Shhh, Will. This is for my Western civ class."

Will's tawny face split into a grin. "You're watching a *movie* for a history class?"

George nodded. "We're studying the French Revolution," she explained. "The professor thought this was good background material, so when he passed out a few copies, I grabbed one and—"

"And I'm going to grab you," Will growled, crawling playfully on top of her.

"Will . . ." George said. She grabbed his black ponytail, tipped back his head, and gave him a level stare. Will was tall and thin and had the most beautiful brown eyes she'd ever seen. "I'm busy, Will," she told him gently. "Really. I can only watch this tape tonight, because we're discussing it tomorrow."

Abruptly, Will rolled off her. "Okay," he said sullenly.

"Will," George said. "You're taking this personally."

Will shrugged. "I know what you're worried about. And look, I admit it, I wish you weren't worried about that."

George tensed. The week before, for several long days, George had the worst scare of her life. She'd thought she was pregnant.

As it turned out, it had been a false alarm, and

when she finally told Will about her ordeal, he was sympathetic—even willing to call off the sexual side of their relationship until she worked out her feelings.

So why was he suddenly acting as if he'd forgotten everything they'd talked about? George fumed. Didn't he get it?

"I miss you, George," Will said. "You've been so busy the last few days. Don't you have even a few extra minutes to spare for me?"

"A *few* minutes?" George rolled her eyes. "I know you well enough to know we're not talking about a few minutes."

"Let me just put my arms around you," Will began, slipping his hand around her waist.

George felt herself flinch involuntarily. "Just let me watch the movie," she snapped before she could stop herself.

It was Will's turn to flinch.

"I can't believe you're still obsessing about getting pregnant!" he shot back.

George shook her head. She didn't want to have to go over all this again. "I don't think *obsess* is the right word, Will," she said finally.

"Then what is the right word?"

"I need time out, Will," George said with a sigh. Her eyes were glued to the television screen. It was so hard for her to explain her feelings, especially since she felt so alone.

Her best friends, Nancy and Bess, hadn't made this leap with a guy yet. Getting intimate with Will had seemed right at the time, but now . . .

George sighed again as she looked at her boyfriend slumped against the back of the couch, his arms folded angrily across his chest. A month ago she'd thought sex would bring them closer than ever. Now it seemed as if it was tearing them apart.

CHAPTER 2

Nancy, you've been glued to your computer for the past three hours!" Nancy's roommate, Kara Verbeck, complained.

"Really?" Nancy couldn't believe it. She stopped typing her paper for Western civ and glanced at her watch. Sure enough, it was eleven o'clock. She had been sitting there for three straight hours. But the good news was that she'd nearly finished the paper.

"Maybe you should do some stretching exercises," Kara suggested. She was sitting in a lotus position on the floor of their room in Thayer Hall, nibbling on a whole-wheat cracker. "Come on. Relax for a while."

Nancy scrolled through her document, then gave the spell-check button a punch. "Finishing a term paper a week early—now, that's relaxing."

Kara rolled her eyes.

Nancy sat back in her desk chair as thoughts

of Bess and Ned flooded back into her mind. All those years together, she thought. We were friends. All of us. And now the two of them were involved. The worst part was the way she'd found out—by bursting in on them.

"I'm going out to the lounge to get something to drink," Kara said. "Do you want to come?"

"No thanks." Nancy shook her head.

She sat in front of her computer for a while longer, first proofreading, then printing out the paper. As she stood up to head to the hallway to get a snack from the vending machine, the telephone rang.

"Hello?"

"Um, Nancy?" came a familiar voice. "It's Bess. Look, I—"

Anger sparkled inside of Nancy. Before she could think of what to do or say, she slammed the receiver down into the cradle. Then she stared at it in shock. For the first time in her life, she'd hung up on Bess.

RRRRRIIIIIINNNGGGG.

The phone rang again. Nancy ignored it, and it finally stopped.

"Are you okay?" said a voice from the hallway. "You don't look so great, and I've been knocking very politely on your door for several minutes without getting an answer."

Nancy groaned inwardly as she turned toward the door. The last person she wanted to see was Stephanie Keats—the biggest flirt on campus.

"Sooo," Stephanie said, striding into the room, "what's going on?"

"Nothing," Nancy said firmly. She wasn't about to spill her problems with Bess and Ned to Stephanie. "I've just been working on my Western civ paper. That's all."

"Oh, really?" Stephanie said, raising her eyebrows. She didn't look as if she believed Nancy, but she was fiddling nervously with the zipper on her skintight leather jumper, as if she had something on her own mind.

"So what's up with you?" Nancy asked before Stephanie could ask more questions.

Stephanie hesitated, then blurted out, "Actually, I need advice."

Nancy was surprised. She and Stephanie weren't exactly best friends. "From me?"

"Yes." Stephanie nodded. "You're the perfect person to discuss my problem with," she said. She splayed her left hand on her thigh and began examining her long red nails. "You know how to hang on to a guy. Long-term, I mean."

"I do?"

Stephanie shrugged. "I know you just broke up with Jake. But you were with him forever."

"It was only a couple of months, Stephanie," Nancy reminded her.

But Stephanie had her eyes closed, as if she hadn't heard. "And before you came to Wilder, you were with that cute Ned Nickerson for *years.*"

Nancy's throat tightened. Stephanie was right

14

about that. She had been with Ned for a long time.

"And what I want to know," Stephanie went on, "is how did you do it? How could things stay perfect for that long?"

"Perfect?" If Nancy hadn't felt so miserable, she would have laughed. "Things were definitely not perfect with Ned," she said. "They weren't perfect with Jake either."

Stephanie stood up. "Well, I want things to be perfect with Jonathan," she explained. "It's just . . ." Her words trailed off as she began pacing the room. "I can't seem to remain faithful to him."

This time Nancy did smile, though she turned away to hide it from Stephanie. Stephanie's ongoing adventures with the best-looking guys on the Wilder campus were legendary in Thayer Hall.

"So, how did you keep those relationships from cracking?" Stephanie asked. "I love Jonathan. I really do. But . . . well, every time I see a cute guy, I can't help flirting with him. It's like, I have to have him."

Nancy turned to face her. Stephanie really did sound sincere. "I think you need to make a commitment, Steph. Decide what you really want, then stick with it."

"What do you mean?" Stephanie asked.

Nancy cleared her throat. "What I mean is, if Jonathan's really the one you love, then put your whole heart into keeping him—forever."

"I get it," Stephanie said, her eyes brightening.

"I just have to make up my mind about Jonathan's being the one, then focus on it."

"Right." Nancy tried to smile, but tears had formed in her eyes as Stephanie played back her words.

Why hadn't she followed her own advice?

"Bess?"

"Hi, Ned," Bess said quietly, twisting the phone cord around her fingers and staring at a huge pile of unstudied biology notes.

"Just wanted you to know that I got back safely last night," Ned went on cheerfully.

"Great," Bess replied.

"Hey," Ned joked, "you don't sound glad. Long day of classes or something?"

Bess hesitated. A part of her wanted to keep her problems with Nancy to herself. She kept telling herself the whole misunderstanding would blow over sooner or later. But it was so incredibly painful to know that she'd hurt Nancy, and that Nancy was still furious with her.

"Actually, I'm pretty upset," Bess confessed. "I called Nancy last night."

There was a pause on the other end of the line. "So—what did she say?"

"She didn't say anything," Bess went on. "She hung up on me."

"She hung up on you?" Ned sounded shocked. "Whoa."

"She must be really angry," Bess blurted out.

"I knew she misunderstood what was going on in my room last night."

"I don't get it," Ned said. "I mean, she's the one who broke up with me. What does she care if the two of us were hugging?"

"It was probably a big shock to see us like that," Bess said. "You guys went out for a long time, and now she thinks I'm dating you."

"But we're not dating!" Ned broke in, frustrated.

Bess felt a pang. "No, we're not," she made herself say.

"So all you have to do is tell her."

"She hung up on me—remember? I haven't had the chance," Bess replied.

"Right," Ned said.

Bess talked to Ned for a few more minutes, but by the time they hung up, he sounded distant and antsy.

Tears filled her eyes. Eventually she'd sort out things with Nancy, but it was different with Ned. There would always be a barrier between Ned and Bess—and her name was Nancy Drew.

Ned slowly placed the phone back on its hook. "Who are you angry with, Nan?" he whispered. "Bess or me?"

Abruptly, he scooped up a basketball from his desktop and took a shot at the hoop attached to the back of the door. He knew Nancy well enough to know that she'd never hang up on anyone unless she was angry—really angry.

But why would it bother her so much to see me hug someone else? he thought for the hundredth time. Nancy had been the one to break up with him. And she'd been the one who'd had a serious boyfriend since their breakup.

Ned picked up the ball again. He could see Nancy's beautiful face and blue eyes so clearly, it was as if she were right in the room with him. He bounced the ball once, then sunk it into the basket. He could feel his heart racing as if he'd just played a real game on a full-length court.

Were things *really* over between him and Nancy—or had this just been a temporary separation?

"Shut off that printer," Gail Gardeski, editor-in-chief of the *Wilder Times,* ordered. "And pull up some chairs. We've got a meeting to get under way and I don't have time to waste."

Nancy gulped down the last of her coffee and got ready to listen. She'd joined the newspaper shortly after arriving on campus and she really enjoyed it.

"I want Blackburn to cover the university regents' meeting tonight," Gail said, ignoring the groan from the back of the room. Nobody ever liked covering the regents' meetings—they were usually pretty boring. "Jampolski—check out that new fitness test over at the health center."

Nancy sat on the edge of her seat as Gail continued barking out her rapid-fire assignments. Inside the busy office, phones rang. Fax machines whined. E-mail message lights blinked.

"Nancy," Gail continued quickly, scanning the list in front of her. "We need something on the men's cross-country team."

Nancy sat up. "Great. The cross-country team is hot this year."

"Yeah," someone in the back spoke up. "Athletics brought in a dynamo new coach and he's started turning things around."

"Right." Nancy nodded. "Chuck Hayes. Since he took over this year, the team's won three straight meets."

"Yeah, yeah," Gail went on distractedly. "Everyone got psyched, except me, of course. I've got other things to worry about." Gail gave Nancy a smile. "But I know that *you* can get into this one, right, Drew?"

Nancy grinned and gave her the thumbs-up sign. It would be fun to cover a sports story, after her last few assignments, which had been on the math club and a controversy over spending more money to upgrade computers. Plus, Nancy had heard that Coach Hayes was some kind of motivational wizard who'd completely turned the team around. Last year the school's cross-country team had placed last in nearly every meet they'd entered.

"Good," Gail said, digging through a file folder. "Here are some interview prospects."

Nancy snatched a slip of paper and scanned the list of names. It included the new coach, a star freshman runner, Rick Alexander, and someone named Judd Wright. "Looks good," she said.

Gail nodded. "We'll use it as a feature for the Sunday issue, week after next. So have two thousand words on my desk a week from Wednesday."

"Okay," Nancy said, clutching the slip of paper. Gail didn't know it, but the assignment was exactly what she needed to help her forget her troubles with Ned and Bess.

George pushed open the glass door to Java Joe's and breathed in the rich aromas of coffee beans and homemade muffins. Her Tuesday afternoon calculus class was over, and she was seriously considering a five-mile run before dinner.

"I want an orange-pineapple smoothie," George told the cashier.

"Cool," a voice behind her said. "I'll have that, too. Hi, George."

George turned and smiled. "Hey, Nikki." Nikki Bennett was a friend of Nancy's roommate, Kara. Her long black hair was pulled back into a tight ponytail, revealing silver earrings. Her slender body was swathed in a gauzy tunic top.

The girls grabbed their drinks and walked over to a nearby table. "Sit down and tell me about your latest talk-show exploits," George said.

Nikki laughed. She and two friends hosted a popular call-in show at the campus radio station. The show always made George laugh—the topics were usually pretty ridiculous, like "What's Your

Favorite Jell-O Flavor and Why?" or "What's Your Favorite First-Date Campus Hang-out?"

"Exploits?" Nikki repeated, rolling her eyes. "Give me a break. Lately we've been desperate for topics."

George grinned. "I wondered if you guys were scraping the bottom of the barrel when you invited the entire university football team to field questions about their love lives."

"Pretty shallow—huh?" Nikki said. She sipped her drink. "I've been thinking of doing some more important topics—things that women especially want to discuss."

"Yeah," George cracked, "like tips on getting your boyfriend out of your hair during midterm week?"

"No." To George's surprise, Nikki actually looked serious. "Shows about important issues like pregnancy prevention, date rape, and how to prepare for a career. That sort of thing."

"I hear you," George said. "That sounds great."

"I've decided that we spend way too much time talking about men in the show," Nikki went on. "Women need to focus on themselves and stop worrying about having a boyfriend all the time."

"You're onto something there," George said softly. She couldn't help but remember her earlier conversation with Will and how casually he'd treated her pregnancy scare. He'd acted as if she was being neurotic and it was no big deal.

Nikki leaned forward conspiratorially. "Actually, I'm doing some research on a few women's issues tomorrow night. I'm going to a meeting of the university's women's group, the Sekhmet Society."

"The *what?*" George wrinkled her nose.

Nikki shrugged. "The Sekhmet Society. It has something to do with an Egyptian lion-goddess, but it's just a name. What's important is that the meeting is just women talking about issues important to women. Why don't you come, George?"

George hesitated, then found herself nodding. "Actually it sounds pretty interesting. I'll come— as long as I have time to squeeze in a five-mile run before—"

George suddenly remembered something. "Whoops. I almost forgot. I can't go—I've got a date with Will tomorrow night to see that new high-explosive spy movie."

"That guys' movie?" Nikki shook her head. "See, this is a perfect example of what we've been talking about. Would you actually go to that movie on your own? Is that your idea of a good time?"

"Not really." George sat back and ran her fingers through her short curls. "Point taken," she said slowly. Nikki had made her think. Maybe her problems with Will boiled down to all the little compromises she'd made along the way in their relationship. Maybe that's why Will wasn't taking her seriously now, when she really needed to take a stand on something important.

"You're on," George finally told Nikki. "What time is the meeting?"

Nikki grinned. "Seven."

By the time George stood up a few minutes later, she was pretty excited about attending the meeting of the Sekhmet Society. A women's group was just what she needed right now.

Bumping into Nikki had been a stroke of luck.

CHAPTER 3

Jonathan reached across the candlelit table and stroked Stephanie's cheek.

Stephanie sighed. She loved sitting and staring into Jonathan's eyes, watching him admire her.

"You look so beautiful tonight," Jonathan went on. "I love it when you wear that black dress."

"I always wear it when we go to Marcel's," Stephanie whispered.

"Maybe that's why I like to take you here, even though I can't afford it," Jonathan joked.

Stephanie felt herself melting all over again. It was astounding to her that she could still feel this way after weeks of dating Jonathan. There was something kind and reassuring about him that made her feel so good.

She felt a pang of guilt that made her look down suddenly at her menu. What had she been doing last night in the library with that guy with the ponytail—whatever his name was?

"Let's splurge," Jonathan said. "Filet mignon?"

"Perfect," Stephanie said. She pushed the guilty thoughts out of her head and found herself wishing that the evening could last forever. The two of them at Marcel's, gazing into each other's eyes. No studying or work. No distractions like . . .

"Are you ready to order?" Stephanie heard a voice murmuring pleasantly into her right ear.

She looked up. The waiter stood there, flashing a perfect smile. He had dark intriguing eyes and closely cropped hair. He's great-looking, she thought.

"We'd both like the filet mignon," Jonathan was saying. "Medium rare, with baby potatoes on the side and blue cheese dressing on our green salads."

The waiter smiled again, this time at Stephanie. "Sounds like you two know what you like."

"Oh, yes." Stephanie swallowed hard. At least I think I know what I want, she thought as she watched the handsome waiter head back toward the kitchen. The waiter had such deep-set eyes and was so sure of himself—suddenly she could imagine running off with him, maybe to the European estate his family had held for generations. . . .

"I got a raise today," Jonathan said, interrupting her fantasy.

Stephanie looked up in surprise. "You did?" she managed to say.

Jonathan looked sheepish for a second. "Well,

I'm afraid the management of Berrigan's Department Store couldn't part with a great deal of cash. But it was a raise, anyway."

Stephanie watched his face. Jonathan looked so happy and proud. "Good for you," she said, reaching across the table and squeezing his hand. "You're going places, Jonathan."

"Thanks, Steph. I hope so. I mean, I'll be working there, and . . ."

As Jonathan went on, Stephanie found herself remembering Nancy's advice from the day before. "I think you need to make a commitment. Decide what you really want and . . ."

Nancy's right, Stephanie thought. I do need to make a commitment. And the person to commit to was sitting right in front of her. Jonathan Baur.

Stephanie caressed his hand. She felt so grown up and secure when she was with him. He treated her like an adult, a grown woman—totally opposite from the way her father treated her.

Stephanie could feel herself getting upset just thinking about her father. He acted as if she were still twelve years old.

Now, Dad is someone who knows zero about commitment, Stephanie thought bitterly. Her millionaire father was divorced from her mom, and he was newly married to a bubble-brain named Kiki.

"Oh, Benjamin!" a blond woman in her twenties suddenly let out an excited scream, interrupting Stephanie's thoughts.

She watched as the woman jumped up and

threw her arms around the man across the table from her and began crying.

When the embrace finally broke up, the guy turned to everyone and raised his glass. "Hey, everyone. We just got engaged!"

The deliriously happy woman wiped her eyes and realizing that everyone was looking at her, held up her left hand. Stephanie saw a large diamond engagement ring sparkling on her finger.

"Congratulations," Jonathan called out as the rest of the crowd clapped.

Stephanie clapped, too. How romantic, she thought wistfully. This couple was so much in love they knew they wanted to be together for the rest of their lives. Now *that's* commitment, Stephanie thought.

Just then the waiter set down their salads. As Stephanie lifted her fork, she gazed at the engaged couple again. Suddenly an idea popped into her mind, an idea so brilliant and right that she couldn't believe it had taken her so long to think it up.

She gave Jonathan a radiant smile. At last she had the answer to her problems.

"I vote for Guy Number Two," Kara Verbeck was saying the next afternoon, her green eyes glued to the television screen in the Thayer Hall third-floor dorm suite. "He likes windsurfing—and he's into women who can take care of themselves."

"Yeah." Ginny Yuen looked up from her advanced calculus notebook. "But Guy Number Three has an actual job," she pointed out sensibly.

"Guy Number Three is definitely better material," Liz Bader agreed. She reached into a large bag of potato chips. "Deep down, under all that muscle, the windsurfer is a lump."

Nancy dragged the potato-chip bag away from Liz and settled it into her lap. She stared silently at the shampoo commercial following *The Mating Game*. It had been a long day of classes. She knew she should be doing something productive, like working on the essay she had due in her English lit class or cleaning out her drawers, but all she wanted was to be a total couch potato.

She couldn't stop thinking about Ned—and about Bess. And about the two of them together.

"Nancy?"

Nancy looked over.

Kara was looking at her suspiciously. "Nancy. You're not hearing me."

"Yeah," Ginny agreed. "What's up? I've never seen you sit still for so long."

Nancy shrugged. "It's nothing."

"I don't believe you," Liz said. She pushed the Off button on the television remote and focused on Nancy.

Nancy looked at her friends. So far she hadn't told a soul about the scene she'd walked into the other night. But they knew something was up and it was obvious she couldn't keep it a secret much longer. "Okay. It's Bess." She paused. "And Ned."

"Ned?" Kara repeated. "What do you mean—Bess and Ned?"

"Bess and *Ned?*" Liz looked shocked.

Nancy shrugged. "I guess so. I mean, I think so. I mean, it *looks* like it."

Nancy felt tears stinging her eyes again. "I saw them together the night before last in Bess's room," she said, taking a deep breath. "They were just hugging, but . . ."

"But what?" Ginny prodded her.

Nancy bit her lip. "They looked so . . . intimate or something," she said, trying to find the right word for what she'd seen. "Like they were more than friends. And when they spotted me"—Nancy shook her head—"they sprang apart, as if they were guilty of something."

"I thought Ned still cared for you," Ginny said quietly.

"I don't think so," Nancy admitted. "He was here all weekend and avoided me the whole time." She paused. "Ned and Bess have gotten really close since Paul died. It's natural. . . ." She trailed off, unable to continue.

"It must have hit a nerve," Ginny said sympathetically.

"A nerve?" Kara cried. "Are you kidding? I'd go nuts if I saw my best friend with my old boyfriend!"

"But, Kara," Liz said sensibly, "be reasonable." She turned to Nancy. "You broke up with

29

Ned a long time ago. You told me yourself you'd fallen out of love with him."

Nancy leaned forward and cradled her face in her hands. "Yeah, I know I did."

"And even if there was something going on between Bess and Ned," Liz reasoned, "why should it matter to you?"

"You're about as emotional as a telephone pole sometimes, Liz," Kara complained.

"But Liz does have a point," Ginny said. "Maybe Nancy has more feelings for Ned than she realizes."

A pang went through Nancy as Ginny said exactly what she'd been thinking for the past couple of days.

"I think you need to cut loose and have a little fun," Liz went on. "Since you and Jake broke up, your phone hasn't exactly been ringing off the hook."

"She's been busy with schoolwork and the paper," Kara defended her.

"That's fine," Liz said. "But it's our responsibility as her friends to see that she has fun, too."

Nancy nodded, glad she'd confessed her feelings to her friends. Liz was right—she did need to get out and have more fun.

"I'm going to Wilder's first home track meet at Holliston Stadium tomorrow to get some background for an article—you guys want to come?" Nancy said.

Liz grinned. "That's not exactly my idea of fun, but it's a good start."

Nancy smiled back. "So, what do you say we get out there and root for the Norsemen!"

By four o'clock the next afternoon, Holliston Stadium was buzzing with excitement. The field was filling up with cross-country fans.

A large banner had been strung across downtown Weston's Main Street wishing the team good luck. Nancy knew that the local newspaper had also run a big story and color photo on the team's rising star, Judd Wright.

"Talk about an unbelievable season," George said over the noise as Nancy, George's roommate Pam Miller, Liz, and Kara followed the stream of bodies toward the bleachers. "Last year they were ranked at the bottom of their division, but this year they might win the title."

Nancy gazed out over the field. The athletes were scattered over the turf, bending into their stretching routines.

"Chuck Hayes is a really incredible coach," Pam said, crossing her long legs. Like George, Pam was an athlete and a runner.

"Yeah, I read somewhere that his last team broke all kinds of records," Liz chimed in. "In fact, I think they came close to the national championships."

Nancy nodded. "Wilder was really lucky to get him."

Pam suddenly nudged Nancy. "That's Judd Wright—the tall runner in the second lane."

"The cute blond guy in the middle of the hamstring stretch?" Liz asked. "He's the star runner?"

Nancy nodded. "His times are so good he could end up in the next Olympic tryouts. And he's only a sophomore."

Her eyes stayed riveted to Judd Wright's lean torso and long muscular legs. As he rose from his stretch, she could see that he had a tanned face and bright intelligent eyes.

To her surprise, she found herself eager to interview him.

"I take it back, Nancy," Liz teased her. "This *is* fun."

A second later Pam pointed to a very thin dark-haired guy who was pacing back and forth in the fourth lane. "That's Rick Alexander." The runner's hands were on his hips and he was staring intently up at the sky as if he were concentrating very hard. "He's really hot," Pam went on. "And *he's* only a freshman at Wilder."

"Oh, there's Bess!" George suddenly shouted, standing up and waving at the stadium entrance.

Nancy stiffened. This was the first time that she'd bumped into Bess since she'd caught her friend with Ned. As Bess waved and headed toward them, Nancy abruptly stood up. She just wasn't ready to face Bess or act as if everything between them was fine. "I'm going to grab a cup of tea and go sit in the press box," she said quickly. "I'll catch you later."

Her friends looked at her, surprised. Before

any of them could say anything, though, Nancy had made her escape.

Bess maneuvered through the crowd of spectators.

"I'm glad to see you guys," Bess said, dropping down next to George and the others. "Am I late?"

Liz and Kara exchanged looks.

"Actually," Liz said with a wry smile, "I think your timing's perfect."

"What do you mean?" Bess asked.

"You just missed Nancy," Kara explained.

Bess flinched.

"She's doing a big feature story for the *Times* on the cross-country team," George explained. She looked at Kara and Liz, then back at Bess. "It was strange, but she bolted right before you got here."

Bess bit her lip. "Nancy hasn't talked to you, has she?"

"Talked to me about what?" George asked.

Bess sighed. "Nancy won't talk to me," she started. "When she walked into my room on Monday, Ned was hugging me goodbye. I guess she took it the wrong way, because"—Bess swallowed—"when I called to explain she hung up on me."

"She hung up on you?" George repeated.

"Nancy thinks Ned and Bess are in love," Liz said bluntly.

George's jaw dropped. "That's ridiculous!"

Bess nodded, then looked down at her feet.

"Bess!" George grabbed her cousin by the shoulders. "It's not true—is it?"

"No . . ." Bess managed, hoping her cousin wouldn't read the truth in her eyes.

"Good," George said, visibly relieved. Then she slipped an arm around Bess's shoulders. "Nancy will come around. You'll see, this whole thing will blow over by tomorrow."

Liz nodded. "Track her down after the meet," she said. "If you tell her there's nothing going on between you and Ned, you'll clear the air."

Bess nodded and tried to smile. "Thanks, Liz, that's good advice."

"Nancy has been a little strung out since she broke up with Jake," George said suddenly.

"Maybe breaking up with Jake made her think more about Ned," Liz theorized.

Bess sighed. "It was the beginning of the end for Jake when he took that trip home with her to River Heights. He couldn't see why Nancy had such trouble with her dad's new girlfriend. But Ned did. Ned understood perfectly."

"You know, I don't think Nancy's really gotten over Ned," Liz murmured.

George nodded. "I agree."

As the two of them and Kara continued to discuss Nancy's feelings toward Ned, Bess sat thinking. Liz *had* given her sound advice and she would take it. She'd find Nancy right after the meet and finally clear the air.

* * * * *

"Oh man!" a reporter in the press box next to Nancy yelled, thrusting his fist into the air. The stadium was suddenly filled with the sound of screaming fans. "Judd Wright *nailed* that race."

"He just broke the university record!" another reporter shouted

Nancy stood up, too, shouting and applauding with the rest of the crowd. It had been a wild race, with Judd back a place until the last few seconds, when he'd kicked into a powerful sprint that sent him over the finish line in first place.

She stared in awe as Judd slowly walked around the track. His upturned face looked as joyful as anything Nancy had ever seen.

"ALL RIGHT, NORSEMEN!" the crowd cheered.

Nancy grabbed her notebook and hurried out of the press box and onto the field. She was determined to track down Judd Wright and the other runners for her story.

It took only a few moments to spot Judd because he was so tall. He was talking intently with a fit, handsome man wearing gray U of Wilder sweats. Nancy recognized Coach Hayes from photographs she'd seen in the paper. He gave Judd a warm smile and a pat on the back before turning away.

"Um, excuse me," Nancy called out.

Judd turned. "Hi," he said with a curious smile once he spotted Nancy.

Nancy smiled back.

"Do you have a minute?" she asked. "I'm

Nancy Drew from the *Wilder Times.* I'm doing a story on the team."

"Sure." Judd pointed over his shoulder with his thumb. "You should talk to the coach, too. He was just giving me a few pointed criticisms."

"I doubt that," Nancy replied. "Coach Hayes was probably extremely pleased with your performance."

Judd's blue eyes were serious for a minute. "Yeah," he admitted. "I had a good time in the race—but it wasn't the world record. At least not yet."

Nancy dug her notepad out of her shoulder bag. "Is that for the record?" she asked, scribbling down the quote.

"Sure." Judd's expression brightened. "I bet my buddy Rick Alexander will give you some good stuff for the article, too. He just about blew by me today."

"I know." Nancy nodded. "I was hoping you'd introduce me."

Immediately Judd turned away and shouted to a thin runner across the field.

He jogged over.

"This is Nancy Drew," Judd said. "She's doing an article for the paper."

"Hi," Rick said, trying to catch his breath.

"Great race," Nancy said, shaking his hand. She was surprised to see that Rick's pale face was still drenched with sweat. He still seemed a little shaky and out of breath.

"Looking good out there, bud," Judd was telling Rick.

Rick shook his head a little. "Whew. I'm wiped."

Nancy ran her eyes down the list of interview questions she'd prepared. "Tell me a little about your new coach. Do you credit him with your team's turnaround?"

Before Judd and Rick could answer, she felt a movement behind her.

Nancy turned to look. A familiar face, framed by long blond hair, hovered nearby. Nancy blinked in surprise. What was Bess doing there while she was in the middle of an interview?

"Nancy," Bess murmured. "I know you're busy, but I need to talk to you. Can we meet later at the main exit? I'll wait there until you're finished," Bess added.

Nancy's whole body felt tense. She gave a short nod, then turned back to face the runners. Before she looked away she noticed the worried expression in Bess's eyes.

"So," Nancy said, trying to hide how flustered she was. "How about your coach? Is it really true he's a good motivator?"

Nancy thought she saw Judd hesitate, but she was still so distracted by Bess's sudden appearance that she wasn't sure about what she'd seen in his eyes. Judd nodded. "The coach certainly likes to win," he said, "and that's a powerful motivator for the team."

Nancy jotted down his words so she could

quote them. "I've heard that Coach Hayes has become an active volunteer in the Weston community—at the high school and in the Special Olympics program. He sounds like a great guy."

"He's really something," Rick said. "Coach Hayes has more energy than all of us combined."

Judd was silent.

"Well, whatever he did to help you guys, it certainly showed today." After another few minutes, she thanked them and ended the interview. Rick jogged off, but Judd lingered for a few minutes.

"Let me know if you need anything else," he said, tugging the ends of a towel around his neck. "I mean, if you have questions about times and techniques, stuff like that, I'm sure I can help."

"Thanks. That would be great," Nancy said. "Maybe we can meet for coffee tomorrow afternoon?"

Judd's blue eyes brightened. "I'd like that. I'm in the student directory," he went on. "So just give me a call later and we can pick a time."

"Great," Nancy said. "Talk to you later then."

Judd jogged off and Nancy slowly tucked her notebook in her pack and started for the exit where Bess was waiting. She was dreading this conversation with Bess. She didn't want to hear Bess telling her about how close she and Ned were—even if they were still only friends. Nor did she want to discuss her feelings about Ned with Bess. Especially since she was still sorting through them herself.

Every time she thought about Bess in her old boyfriend's arms, she felt a fresh wave of hurt and humiliation.

Nancy stopped for a second to think before she wheeled around and ducked through another exit.

Sorry, Bess, she thought. But I'm not ready to deal with this right now.

CHAPTER 4

I'm going to take notes," Nikki confided to George as they walked up to the front door of the off-campus bungalow where the Sekhmet Society meetings were held. "I bet I'll have lots of new talk-show ideas once I've learned more about the group."

George nodded. She was looking forward to hearing some new ideas, too. She was hoping this group could help her sort through her problems with Will.

As Nikki and George entered the living room, George saw that it was lit entirely by candles, which were perched on every available ledge and tabletop. A group of a dozen or so women sat cross-legged on the rug in front of the hearth.

"Welcome," one of the women said, standing up and smiling. She was slim, with a dark braid and large silver earrings. "I'm Althea Crane, a political science major at Wilder."

"I'm Nikki Bennett," Nikki said quickly. "And this is my friend George."

"George," Althea echoed, her smile broadening. "I like that." She turned and pointed to a large sculpture in the corner of the room depicting the head of a lioness. "This is Sekhmet. She was the goddess of war and battle in ancient Egyptian culture. And while we don't advocate violence, we believe she represents the power and fierceness we are seeking as women."

"Oh." George wasn't sure what to say to that. Finally she smiled, then sat quietly on the rug next to Nikki.

"We start each meeting with what we call check-in," Althea explained. "Each woman around the circle has a chance to tell us anything that's happened in her life over the past week. After that, we discuss a topic we chose the week before. Tonight's discussion is based on the book *Mourn No More: A Woman Alone.*"

This time George had to choke back a giggle. Why were these women reading a book titled *Mourn No More: A Woman Alone?* It sounded ridiculous.

"Isabella was just finishing her check-in," Althea prompted the woman next to her, who had a high pale forehead and soulful eyes.

George gazed around the room, which was also decorated with hanging crystals, flowering plants, and large posters of Virginia Woolf.

"Yes, thank you," Isabella said quietly. "Anyway, I finally decided to break away from Jim. In fact, I moved out yesterday."

A joyful gasp rose up from the group, and several women crawled forward to give Isabella hugs.

Tears streamed down Isabella's face. When they all took their places again, she took a deep breath. "I was suffocating," she said in a trembling voice. "Jim thought he loved me, but I realize now that he didn't. Jim loved the beauty and love and support I brought into his life. But not me for myself."

"Your needs were always secondary!" a woman near the window blurted out. She stood up and began pacing. "What if you'd gotten pregnant like I did? I bet Jim would have laughed it off—or walked, just like David did."

George stiffened.

"You're right," Isabella said tearfully, her eyes angry.

"Why do we bother?" another woman with very short blond hair burst out. "Men bring pain into our lives. Nothing but pain. We'd be better off living with cats."

Althea let out a bitter laugh. "You can't get pregnant living with a cat, that's for sure."

There was a murmur of approval around the circle, and George found herself nodding with the rest of them.

Nikki nudged George in the side. "These women are so supportive of each other," she whispered.

"Even if you *don't* get pregnant," Isabella pointed out, "there's so much risk involved in having the kind of relationship I had with Jim." She looked around the group, her eyes intent. "Men can drain you emotionally, and then make you forget who you are."

George bit her lip. At first the stuff about the lioness had seemed kind of weird. But now she liked what these women were saying. They were voicing many of the same worries George had when she thought about having sex again with Will.

Sure, she loved Will. But he consumed a lot of her time—time she needed to study and focus on school. Plus, there was the very real possibility that she could get pregnant. George didn't want to go through that scare again.

As another woman started to speak, George leaned forward to listen. Suddenly she had the feeling that there was a lot these women could teach her.

"I, Stephanie Keats, do take thee, Jonathan Baur, to be my lawfully wedded husband . . ." Stephanie was murmuring to herself.

She was hurrying down Main Street on her way to Berrigan's, where she was meeting Jonathan for their date. Reciting wedding vows wasn't her usual routine. But ever since the night before, when she'd watched the couple at Marcel's announce their engagement, she'd been thinking about wedding cakes. Bridal gowns. Picturesque wedding chapels. Sparkling diamond rings.

"Mrs. Jonathan Baur," Stephanie said to herself. "Stephanie Baur. Mr. and Mrs. Jonathan Baur. Stephanie Keats Baur."

She used to think that marriage was boring and for older people. But now, remembering the way that couple had looked, she thought it was incredibly romantic.

Stephanie reached the corner across from Berrigan's. As she began heading across the street, something drew her gaze—Berrigan's store windows, glowing brightly in the dim evening light.

As she walked closer, she saw that the main display window had been decorated in lavish white and silver. Baskets of white flowers lined the front of the window. And in the center of the display was a dark-haired mannequin wearing a stunning, full-length, white satin bridal gown.

Stephanie stared, barely realizing that the Walk had turned to Don't Walk and that a car was honking off to her right. Mesmerized, she glided toward the window.

The gown had a scoop neck and a tight-fitting bodice with tiny buttons running up the front. The veil, which was long and gauzy, was held on with a crown of white roses.

Stephanie suddenly felt off balance and slightly giddy as she stood on the sidewalk, staring. The display was still being put together by an older woman from the third-floor bridal department. Stephanie noticed then that she wasn't alone.

Climbing into the display, carrying a bouquet of roses and a staple gun was—

"Jonathan!" Stephanie gasped softly.

She watched, fascinated, as Jonathan carefully stapled the bouquet into place. Then, as gently as he could, he put his two hands on the bride's waist and moved her slightly to the right.

Stephanie's knees felt weak. It was as if she were watching a movie of herself. There was Jonathan, and there was the bride. It was uncanny. First the couple at Marcel's. And now Jonathan with the bride in the window.

A shiver ran through Stephanie as she stood silently on the sidewalk. The setting sun had suddenly dropped below a bank of clouds, sending bright gold light into the street. The gold light flooded Berrigan's window.

"It's a sign," Stephanie said to herself.

The only way she would find happiness with Jonathan and feel better about herself was to make a commitment. A commitment that her father hadn't been able to make to her or her mother, but one that Stephanie was determined to make to Jonathan.

She stood outside, thinking as she watched the sun's last rays give way to darkness. Now all she had to do was find a way to put her plan into action.

"So, you probably want a high protein drink or something," Nancy teased Judd as they entered Java Joe's together. "Being an athlete and all."

"Yuck." Judd made a face. "No thanks."

Nancy laughed as they approached the guy behind the counter. Judd looked different in his plain white T-shirt and jeans. But he was still really friendly. And still really good-looking, she thought. She ordered iced tea while Judd asked for orange juice.

"Athletes aren't the saints you think we are," Judd said as they sat down at a nearby table. He unloaded his heavy pack and pulled out a chair opposite Nancy's.

Nancy drew out her notebook and nodded toward the backpack. "Looks like you're carrying a full course load on top of your cross-country schedule. Is it hard to manage?"

Judd nodded. "I'm on an athletic scholarship," he explained. "So I have to keep up the running and my grades." He grinned. "But I can't live without running, and I can't go to school without the scholarship. So it works out pretty well."

For a minute Nancy's eyes lingered on Judd's wide smile. Before the scene with Bess and Ned she might have been seriously interested in Judd Wright. He was a really nice guy.

Abruptly, she looked down at her pad and wrote down Judd's remark.

"Like that quote, huh?" Judd said.

"Yup." Nancy smiled. "It makes you sound hardworking and dedicated. Maybe that's why you and the rest of the team have improved so much," she went on.

Judd looked surprised. "You've been doing homework," he said with a wry smile. "You must know then that I wasn't so hot last year, and the team lost every one of its meets."

Nancy nodded. "I know that last year your times were fine, but not *this* fine."

"I trained hard all summer," Judd said. "It's amazing what the right kind of weight work and nutrition advice can do."

"And Coach Hayes?" Nancy prompted. "He sounds like he's pretty amazing. What did he do?"

Judd shrugged. "He pushes us."

"It's that simple?" she said skeptically.

Judd took a slow gulp of his juice. "How long did you say you've been a reporter?" he asked. "You're very good, you know."

"Thanks," Nancy replied. "But seriously. What's Coach Hayes's technique like? How does he motivate the runners?"

"He's a hard-driving guy," Judd said, "and he knows a lot about running. He's helped me a lot with my starts, for instance. But, in general, I'd say he's a guy who really wants to win, and that's the greatest motivation there is, I guess."

Nancy wrote down his remarks. "It's obvious that he's been a tremendous influence on the team."

"Yeah," Judd said softly. "It is pretty obvious."

Nancy waited for him to say more, but instead he flashed her a lazy grin. "I've got to get going in a minute. What do you say we continue this interview tomorrow at Club Z. The whole team will be there celebrating our victory. Why don't you check it out with me?"

For a moment, Nancy didn't know what to say. Judd was nice. . . .

But he isn't Ned, came another voice.

Before she could respond to his invitation, Judd folded his arms and looked worried. "Uh-oh. I guess I said the wrong thing."

Nancy shook her head. "Not at all." As Judd gave her another one of his easy smiles, she pushed Ned from her mind. "Actually, Judd, I'd love to go with you."

"The organic compounds present in this rare subspecies are of particular importance to medical researchers in the area of . . ." Bess was reading silently to herself.

It was late Thursday afternoon, and she was trying to concentrate on her biology notes. But it was a real struggle. With a sigh, she reached for the candy bar she'd bought from the machine down the hall. Maybe the sugar would wake her up.

As Bess bit into the chocolate bar, she knew it wouldn't do the trick. Nothing would do the trick.

She had lost her best friend. Nancy Drew. The friend she'd had since childhood. Nancy: the one who'd pulled her out of a thousand jams. The one she looked up to. The friend she would have done anything for.

Bess still couldn't believe that Nancy hadn't shown up at the stadium exit yesterday. How could she blow me off like that? Bess wondered.

Tears began to trickle down her face as she thought about that terrible moment when Nancy had burst into her room. Bess knew she had leaned on Ned a lot after Paul died. . . . But you never should have let yourself get so close to him, she chided herself. Still, the whole thing had been harmless.

Bess wished Nancy would let her explain.

Bess reached for a tissue just as the door to her room flew open. Her roommate, Leslie King, stormed through the door.

"I hate him!" she cried, slamming the door and flinging herself on her bed.

Bess stared, dumbfounded. Strands of Leslie's straight brown hair were sticking out from her ponytail, and her whole body was tense. She looked as if she was furious. Bess had never seen levelheaded premed student Leslie act like this.

"Leslie?" Bess asked. "What happened?"

"I'll say one thing, Bess. Then I won't say anything else. Nathan Kress. That's all. Just Nathan Kress."

"Okay, Les," Bess said quietly. Nathan was Leslie's boyfriend, and they'd obviously had a huge fight. Bess was usually the one who complained about her problems with guys. Tonight it was definitely Leslie's turn.

But Bess's quiet, studious roommate wasn't about to spill her guts. She lay on her bed for a few minutes with her eyes closed, then sat up and grabbed a can of soda off her desk. She popped open the can and took a gulp. Next thing Bess knew, Leslie was humming.

Bess's jaw dropped. That was it? Leslie's fit was over?

Leslie looked at Bess with a cheerful expression. "What's up?"

Bess could barely speak. "What do you mean? What's up with you? You were ballistic a few minutes ago. Now you look like you just aced your med-school entrance exams."

Leslie chuckled, slipping a magazine off her desk. "I'm not *that* happy."

Bess turned over on her side and looked at Leslie intently. "But you're not mad."

"What's the point of staying mad?" Leslie said sensibly. "It'll just spoil my day. Nathan and I will make up later anyway." She threw the magazine down and grabbed her calculus textbook. "Plus, I've got a quiz tomorrow. And I can't study when I'm mad."

"You can just turn it off like that?" Bess asked her.

"Yep," Leslie said, turning to the middle of the text and taking out a yellow highlighter pen.

Bess fell back on her pillow. It's incredible, she thought. While she had spent the past few days agonizing over her problems with Nancy, Leslie had spent exactly two minutes agonizing over her problems with her boyfriend.

Bess stared up at the ceiling. Leslie was right. What was the point? Anger and worry wouldn't heal her friendship with Nancy. Time was probably the only thing that would do that.

What she had to do was get on with her life, Bess told herself.

If she'd learned anything from her blowup with Nancy, it was that there were still strong feelings between Nancy and Ned. Bess wasn't sure what those feelings were. But she knew now that she couldn't put herself in the middle of it.

She and Nancy needed distance, Bess decided. And time.

Leslie knew how to wait out her fights with Nathan. Bess would do her best to follow Leslie's example.

CHAPTER 5

The evening sky had cleared. A full moon shone on the surface of the large pond in Liberty Park, on the outskirts of Weston. Crickets chirped from their hiding spots in the grassy lawn, where Stephanie and Jonathan, bundled up in woolly clothes, lay on a heavy blanket, watching the star-filled sky, and the dying embers of a once blazing fire.

Stephanie felt her heart swell as she slipped her hand into Jonathan's jacket pocket and entwined her fingers with his. "It's so beautiful here."

"I love it, too," Jonathan murmured. "Even if it is kind of late in the season to be outside."

Stephanie propped herself up on her elbow. "I could go on like this forever," she said softly. "Just you and me and the moon and the stars."

Jonathan's expression turned intense. He reached up to stroke the thick strands of her hair that had fallen forward. "You're so beautiful, Stephanie. You're so good for me."

Stephanie's heart skipped a beat. It had only been a couple of hours since she'd had her wedding vision while watching Jonathan in the Berrigan's window display. Talking him into marriage would be the most challenging thing she'd ever done, but she could do it—as long as she kept her cool and played the situation very, very intelligently.

"We're good for *each other*," she said carefully.

Jonathan let out a low chuckle and closed his eyes. "Oh, man, if I'd only known a few months ago how great things were going to get. Here I am with the most beautiful girl I've ever laid eyes on."

Stephanie slid down and curled up under his broad shoulder. "And I love you more than anyone I've ever loved in my life."

Jonathan rolled over on his side, then took her wrists and pinned her gently to the ground on her back, his eyes wide with emotion. "I love you, too, Steph. You've made my life so good."

Stephanie stared up at him, trying to figure out how to make her next move. Behind his face, the stars were twinkling and the few stubborn leaves clinging to the oak trees were rustling in the cold evening breeze. "I've been imagining this moment since I was a little girl," she began, "wondering when I would find my true love and who he would be."

Jonathan laughed softly. "And how he would carry you away on his great white horse?"

"Of course." Stephanie smiled back. "Don't you have a horse?"

"Not really." Jonathan laughed, then got serious again. "Actually it's you who's carried me off. I never want to lose you."

"Likewise." Stephanie snuggled closer. "I can just see us one day," she went on, smiling. "An old married couple sitting on the front porch together, watching the same moon."

"I hope so," Jonathan said.

Stephanie couldn't see his face, but she could tell from his silence that he was thinking hard. She felt certain she had taken the right approach. "I hope so, too, Jonathan."

Jonathan sat up and raked his fingers through his hair. "I can see us in a big city, Steph. We're both in merchandising. We could get jobs. We'd have a blast together."

Stephanie grabbed him and kissed him on the mouth. "Jonathan, are you saying what I think you're saying? I mean, are you talking about you and me—as in a married couple, you and me?"

Jonathan looked at her carefully. "Well," he said slowly, "I guess I am. I hadn't really thought about it until now, but, well, yes, I am. I mean— eventually—I think we should do it." He gazed at her tenderly and cupped her chin in his hand. "I know I'll never find another girl like you, Steph. Never."

Stephanie lay back on the blanket again and

stretched her arms over her head. "Oh, Jonathan." Inside, her mind was whirring.

"What are you thinking, Steph?" Jonathan asked, stroking her hair.

"Well," Stephanie began cautiously. "We know we love each other, and we both know we've found the perfect life partner."

"Yes . . ."

"I—I guess I just wanted you to know," Stephanie said, moving her lips toward Jonathan's ear, "that I would marry you today if you wanted. That's how much I love you."

Jonathan froze and Stephanie held her breath, hoping she hadn't blown it. The expression on his face seemed to flicker back and forth between delight and confusion. "Well—gee, Steph. You would?"

Stephanie nodded, not daring to speak.

Jonathan began to look worried. "This is awfully fast, Steph." He slipped his arm under her back and held her close. "I'm not saying we shouldn't . . ."

"Then what are you saying?" Stephanie said, letting a tear trickle out the side of one eye.

"Well"—Jonathan faltered—"what I'm trying to say is—"

Stephanie sat up and grabbed Jonathan by the shoulders. "Look. I don't want anything to change. I don't want to drop out of school or make you quit your job or leave town or anything like that. I'm an independent person and I always have been. All I'm saying is that I love you and

I want you, Jonathan. I want to wake up every morning and see you there. I want to love you and help you and be your partner in life. And if that's not what you can handle right now, well, then . . ."

Right on cue, Jonathan pulled her to him. "Oh, Stephanie. Of course I want you! You're all I've ever wanted. Whatever you want, baby," he murmured. "That's what we'll do. . . ." Stephanie threw her arms around him and then hungrily sought his lips. As Jonathan kissed her back, he didn't see the triumphant expression in her eyes.

"Judd Wright? The runner with the blond hair?" Kara exclaimed the next morning as Nancy sat in the lounge with friends. "You have a date with Judd Wright?"

Nancy bobbed a tea bag in her cup. "Yep."

"Way to go, Nancy!" Liz exclaimed.

Nancy gave Liz a sly smile. "You were the one who told me to cut loose and start having fun again, Liz. I owe it all to you."

Liz waved her off. "You had to go anyway, as it turns out."

Eileen O'Connor grinned and patted Nancy's hand. "Congratulations. Where are you guys going for this big date tonight, anyway?"

"Club Z," Nancy explained. "The whole team's going to celebrate there."

Eileen snapped her fingers. "That's right. Emmet was telling me that Jason's really gearing up for tonight. The music is going to be great."

Nancy grinned. Eileen's boyfriend was Emmet Lehman, whose brother, Jason, owned Club Z, a hot new dance club downtown. Even though athletic Eileen was usually running or working out with her crew team, she always knew what was hot in Weston. "Why don't you guys come, too?" Nancy said.

"Sounds like a riot," Casey Fontaine joined in, nudging Dawn Steiger and Ginny Yuen. "Come on. We'll go dateless."

"You'd better be dateless, Casey," Kara broke in, laughing. "You're the one who's engaged."

Casey placed a finger on the side of her head, pretending to remember. "Oh, yeah."

Nancy smiled. Casey, Stephanie's roommate, had been a teen star on a hit TV show called *The President's Daughter*. There she'd met actor Charley Stern, and the two had recently decided to get married, though not right away.

"Is someone talking about an engagement?" Stephanie's voice broke in.

Nancy turned as Stephanie strode into the lounge. For eight-thirty in the morning, Stephanie looked incredibly alert, Nancy thought. Her cheeks were glowing, and her dark glossy hair was brushed loose over a black turtleneck dress.

"Oh, it's the usual," Casey said before biting into an apple. "They're all just teasing me about being engaged to Charley. You know, Casey Fontaine—the only engaged girl on the Wilder University campus."

"Actually . . ." Stephanie's lips curved into a smile. "You're not the only one anymore."

Nancy did a double-take. There *was* something different about Stephanie this morning. In fact, Stephanie looked as if she were about to burst.

"Check it out," Stephanie said, suddenly thrusting her left hand out in front of her.

Nancy saw a large man's ring on her fourth finger.

"Stephanie?" Casey gasped. "Are you trying to tell us that—"

"That's exactly what I'm telling you," Stephanie cut in. "Jonathan Baur and I are engaged to be married."

There was a moment of stunned silence.

"Oh, Stephanie," Casey finally said. "I'm so . . . happy for you," she finished.

As the girls all gathered around Stephanie, alarms sounded in Nancy's head. Kind, patient Jonathan was the perfect match for insecure Stephanie, but in her opinion Stephanie was completely unprepared and totally unsuited for marriage. She still had too much growing up to do. Nancy watched as Stephanie sat there, basking in all the attention. Nancy had a lot of objections to Stephanie's news, but she couldn't bring herself to spoil Stephanie's moment of triumph.

"Congratulations," Nancy said instead. "Jonathan's a wonderful guy."

"And so good-looking," Eileen said.

"And patient," Casey chimed in, winking at Stephanie.

"He's a great guy," Dawn added warmly. "Let's see your ring."

"Oh," Stephanie said quickly, looking down at her finger. "Yeah. It's Jonathan's high school class ring. He really wanted me to have it."

"Gee, that's great," Casey said, looking at the clunky man's ring, hastily taped on the underside so it wouldn't fall off Stephanie's finger.

"Yeah," Stephanie replied, stretching her arms up over her head like a contented cat. "Thanks."

"Have you set a date yet?" Nancy asked politely. "Or is it too soon to start thinking about details like that?"

Stephanie dropped her hands in her lap and stared at Nancy. "What are you talking about? Of course we've set a date. We're getting married on . . . Wednesday."

"What?" Nancy blurted out.

"But, Steph," Casey said. "Is that, I mean . . . is that enough time to get ready?"

Nancy was flabbergasted. What on earth was Stephanie doing?

"Sure it's enough time," Stephanie said cheerfully.

"Well, why Wednesday?" Nancy couldn't help asking. "Is it a special day?"

"Yes." Stephanie nodded at Nancy. "Wednesday is perfect, because Jonathan's days off are Thursday and Friday."

Bess hurried out of the cafeteria and headed toward the university clinic, where she had an eight-thirty appointment with her counselor—a psychologist named Victoria Linden.

She'd spent all night tossing and turning, dreading it. Finally she'd turned the light on at six-thirty and studied her biology notes. At least she was getting something done, instead of thinking about Ned and Nancy.

Bess trudged ahead, each step heavier than the last. The weather had gotten cold and she turned up her collar, wondering why she was going to see Victoria at all.

Sure, it had been Ned who'd convinced her to see a counselor after her boyfriend Paul had died. And at first it had been good to talk with Victoria about her guilt and depression.

But lately . . . Bess knew that today Victoria was going to expect her to talk about Ned.

During her last session, she'd told Victoria that Ned was planning a visit. She remembered how Victoria's eyes had narrowed. It was common to become attached to someone who helped you through a crisis, she'd explained. But when your helper was of the opposite sex, Victoria warned, a confusing romantic attachment could follow.

Bess remembered how she had shaken her head and denied it. Ned could never be anything more than a friend to her. And she wasn't confused.

She pressed her lips together and slowed to a stop right in front of the university clinic's steps. Okay, so maybe Victoria was right. Maybe she had fallen in love with Ned. He had been her protector and her confessor and the only person in the world who seemed to know what she needed after Paul died.

But did she really want to spend an hour convincing Victoria that she wasn't planning on acting on her feelings?

"No," Bess said to herself. She didn't want to spend another minute thinking—and worrying— about the situation with Ned Nickerson.

Bess turned on her heel and headed toward Java Joe's instead.

"So what was this women's group called?" Will asking, biting into his burger.

"The Sekhmet Society," George replied, stirring her drink with her straw.

It was Friday noon, and George had just finished a grueling set of classes. She had had a huge paper due in Western civ and a pop quiz in environmental science. Now she and Will were catching a quick lunch at the Cave, a basement snack shop on campus.

Will was smiling. "The *what* society?"

George shifted in her seat. "The Sekhmet Society. It's just a women's group. Sekhmet was an Egyptian warrior goddess."

"Oh." Will wiped his mouth. "So what was it like? I mean, was it stupid—or interesting?"

"Some of it was slightly stupid," George said carefully. "Some of it was good."

"What do women do at one of these things?" he asked, smirking.

"Talk," George shot back.

"About your oppressors?" Will joked, pointing a thumb to his chest. "Us guys."

George shrugged. "Well, some of *you guys* aren't so great. I hate to break it to you, Will, but a lot of women out there have been hurt."

"Okay," Will said, cocking his head to the side. "I'll give you that."

"There was one woman there who was being completely suffocated by this guy she was living with," George told him. "And this other woman, Althea, she's pretty cool."

Will nodded but George saw him sneak a glance at his watch. "Want to go back to my apartment for a while?" he asked as soon as she stopped talking.

George stared at him. "You don't want to hear any of this, do you?"

"Sure I do," Will said good-naturedly. "I just want to hear it over at my place." Will reached under the table and put a hand on George's knee. "Come on. I want to be alone with you," he said softly.

"I can't," George said stonily. "I've got class. If I miss calculus I'll fall hopelessly behind."

"Come on, George," Will coaxed her. "Let's just go home and blow off the rest of the day."

George felt anger stirring in her chest. "I don't need this, Will. First, you start putting down a women's group you know absolutely nothing about—"

"I'm not putting it down," Will jumped in.

"And then you start pressuring me to skip class so that I can have sex with you in your apartment," George continued.

Will just sat there, his jaw set as if he was just as angry as George was.

She stood up abruptly and grabbed her book bag. "I have to go now, Will. I'm sorry, but I just have to go."

"You do what you need to do," Will said coldly. "And that's exactly what I'll do, too."

Without bothering to reply, George whirled around and stomped off. As she headed for the door, she could feel her heart beating fast. The truth was, her professor was planning to review old material in calculus that afternoon, material she already had down cold. She could have easily skipped the class—if she'd wanted to.

It's too soon. I'm not ready for sex so soon after that pregnancy scare, she told herself.

Holding her books tightly against her chest, George ducked through the exit. Outside, the tears finally flowed. Will was a wonderful guy. The best guy in the world. But something was telling her things had gotten too intense too fast. George wanted to slow things down, take time to let herself grow up—even if it meant losing Will, she realized.

CHAPTER 6

Okay, let's go, Bess! Up and at 'em! Focus your energy! Big rehearsal coming up! Come on—" Brian Daglian stopped in midsentence as he opened the door to Bess's dorm room.

Bess looked up from her spot on the floor, which was covered with highlighter pens, papers, notebooks, and a pile of discarded junk food wrappers. "Hi, Brian."

"What are you doing?" he asked, looking around at the mess.

"What do you mean?" she asked.

Brian grinned as he ran his fingers through his short blond hair. "What are you trying to do? Set a world record in calorie consumption?"

Bess let out a sigh. "Well, I have been snacking nonstop," she confessed, "but I've also managed to finish my Western civ term paper, prepare for a quiz in biology, and read three chapters on Freud for psych."

"Pretty impressive," Brian admitted. "Now are you ready to come to rehearsal with me?"

"Rehearsal?" Bess slapped a hand over her mouth, then jumped up. She'd completely forgotten about rehearsal. Next week her class was putting on a one-act play and they were supposed to rehearse all afternoon.

"Carlton, Sandy, and I have all memorized our lines. Have you?" Brian asked.

"Of course. I've memorized everything," Bess told him.

"You're a maniac," Brian said, pushing her gently toward the door.

"Yeah," Bess agreed, glad that Brian didn't have a clue about what was really making her crazy—this situation with Ned and Nancy.

Glad for the chance to concentrate on anything else for a change, she threw on a coat and scarf, grabbed her script, and headed across campus with Brian.

Nancy threw back her head and laughed. She and Judd were squeezed around the band on the Club Z dance floor. The band was a very large, diverse group with twelve drums, three electric guitars, four vocalists, and lots of exotic instruments.

Judd had an arm firmly around Nancy's waist as they bopped to the drums' fast and furious rhythm.

"Having a good time?" Judd asked.

"Yes," Nancy tried to say over the noise. And

it was true. Judd was so fun and easygoing, it was impossible not to like him. He was the perfect casual date, which was exactly what she wanted right now.

"I wish we had these guys pumping us up before each meet," Judd yelled into her ear.

Nancy laughed.

A dancer from the band sprang up onto the stage and began urging the crowd into a wild dance that involved clapping their hands over their heads and mixing kicks, bobs, and steps.

"This is great!" Nancy cried, catching on to the steps and showing Judd.

Over their heads the Club Z dance lights spun and flashed in the darkness. Nancy looked up at the two-story space with high-tech metal stairways and multilevel metal platforms arranged so that every seat faced the huge wooden dance floor below.

Her gaze dropped back to the stage. As it did, she saw a flash of blond hair and a familiar pale blue sweater. Nancy's heart pounded. Was that Bess? Was Ned with her?

Nancy quickly averted her eyes, afraid to know the answer. A few moments later she sneaked another peek. This time as the blond girl turned to face her, she could see that it wasn't Bess.

Whew.

Nancy breathed a huge sigh of relief. It wasn't Bess at all. And there was no Ned.

Why can't I stop thinking about him? she thought in frustration. Here she was with a great guy who seemed to like her, and all she could think about was Ned.

Just then the song changed and Judd reached for her hands and pulled her close. Forget about Ned, a voice inside commanded. He's forgotten all about you.

"Come on, you lioness, you," Will teased, pulling George onto the dance floor as the Club Z band wound down to a slow ballad.

George followed reluctantly. She'd felt so upset and guilty about her blowup at Will earlier that day that she'd called him and suggested a Club Z date.

Now he wrapped his long arms around George and pulled her close. "You feel so good."

Suddenly George wished the band was still playing the fast music.

"Having fun?" Will asked.

George looked up. Will's dark Cherokee eyes glowed above his high cheekbones and his smile was warm and affectionate. She was in love with this guy, wasn't she? Honest, straightforward, loving, caring Will. She'd never felt this way about anyone. So why did she suddenly feel as if they were living in two different galaxies? Did all couples go through this? Or was there something really wrong?

"George, are you okay?" Will asked with concern. "You seem sort of out of it. I thought you wanted to go out tonight."

"Sorry." George was surprised to find the word

sticking in her throat. She didn't want to lie to Will, but he was right. She didn't feel as if she was completely here. She never should have come with him.

As he gave her a kiss, she found herself flashing back to a tip she'd picked up from Althea at the Sekhmet Society meeting. Whenever you want to put some temporary distance between you and your partner, eat a whole clove of garlic. At the time it had seemed like a ridiculous solution, but now it almost seemed like good advice.

As the band took a break, George didn't follow Will back to the table. "I have to go talk to Nancy," she said.

"Oh. Okay," Will replied.

George could hear the disappointment in his voice, but she didn't turn around.

Nancy dropped into a chair near the edge of the dance floor. She'd been dancing for an hour straight. Her muscles were pleasantly tired, but she was parched, and Judd had just left to buy some sodas.

"Hey," she heard George's voice in her ear. "Where's your date?" George asked.

"He's getting some sodas. Where's Will?"

George pursed her lips and waved off the question. She wasn't in the mood to talk about Will right then. "How are things with you and Bess?" she said instead.

It was Nancy's turn to avoid answering. "Forget about it, George. It's between the two of us."

"It's a crazy misunderstanding, Nancy. You two have got to talk."

"Not now," Nancy insisted as the band started a very fast dance number. She wasn't ready to talk and Club Z was definitely not the place to begin.

Suddenly there was a slight movement off to Nancy's right. The noise in the club was deafening, but several people had grouped at the edge of the dance floor, and she could see that they were talking with worried expressions. Someone was bending down, and in the confusion Nancy thought she saw a familiar face.

Ignoring George, Nancy stood up and pushed her way through the bodies. In the distance, she could see the club owner, Jason Lehman, hurrying in their direction, a grim expression on his face.

Nancy finally pushed her way through. Several guys had joined hands to hold back the crowd of dancers to give space to a thin dark-haired guy. He had one knee bent to the floor, and he was shivering and struggling for breath.

Nancy gasped. It was Rick Alexander, the freshman runner whom Judd had introduced to her on the field.

"Rick," someone called out over the din. "What's going on, man?"

Nancy watched in horror as all of the color drained out of Rick's face and he slipped into a cross-legged position on the floor. Sweat began to pour from his forehead.

"Give him more room," Nancy screamed as the crowd pressed in and Rick rolled over onto his side. "Someone call an ambulance!"

"What's going on?" she heard Judd's voice calling out behind her.

Nancy whirled around. "Judd! Rick's collapsed. See if you can get to a phone and call nine-one-one."

"What?" Judd exclaimed, hurrying forward. His head snapped up and he looked sharply at the group of his teammates who were gathered around Rick. "What have you guys been doing?" he shouted.

"George!" Nancy cried out when she realized her friend was at her side. "Ginny Yuen's here. Find her. Fast. She's had a lot of emergency medical training!"

Club Z was so big and crowded, half the people in the place didn't even realize what was happening. Nancy dropped to her knees to loosen Rick's collar and check his pulse.

"Ginny!" Nancy screamed as she spotted George leading their friend toward her.

Ginny knelt down and spoke to Rick. "He's conscious," she yelled over her shoulder, "but struggling to breathe."

"Come on, Rick," someone shouted.

"Try to relax, Rick," Ginny said as she put her ear to his chest. She sat up and looked around. "Has someone called an ambulance?"

"Yeah," two voices shouted back. Jason and

Judd pushed back through the crowd. "It's on its way. What's going on?"

"It's probably his heart," Ginny called back. "The beat is very rapid and irregular."

At that moment Nancy could see that Rick was losing consciousness. His eyes fell back into his head, and he appeared to stop breathing.

"Rick!" Judd cried out. "What did you do to yourself?"

"Everybody, stand back!" Ginny yelled, placing her ear on his chest.

"Get someone outside to flag down the paramedics when they get here!" Nancy cried desperately.

"His heart has stopped," Ginny shouted.

Nancy watched as Ginny placed the heel of one hand on Rick's chest and covered it with the other. She pushed down sharply several times, let up, then slipped her hand under his neck. Propping his head back, Ginny opened Rick's mouth, then blew in two slow puffs of air. Then she quickly tried to start his heart again with several swift thrusts to his chest.

"Come on, Rick," Judd cried out. He reached out to hold his friend's limp hand. "Hang in there, buddy."

Ginny puffed twice again, then pumped his chest again. But Rick's body was like a lifeless weight on the floor.

Just then the music stopped and Nancy heard the whine of a siren.

As Ginny continued CPR, the front double doors of Club Z banged open.

"Over here!" Nancy shouted, waving to the medics who hurried inside.

"We've got heart failure," Ginny yelled. "He's not breathing."

"Cardiac arrest!" one of the paramedics shouted. "Stay with the CPR, we're going to intubate him," he ordered.

Nancy stepped back as the professionals snaked a tube into Rick's throat. By this time, her own heart was beating like a bongo drum.

"Defibrillator! I want thirty watt seconds of energy," one of the paramedics shouted, as the other hurried toward Rick with an electrical device strapped to each hand. "And I want an amp of epinephrine and lidocaine!"

"Okay. Stand back everyone," the second paramedic shouted. Rick's limp body jumped once, then twice.

"Okay, we've got a beat," the paramedic yelled. "Let's get him out of here."

Judd was hanging on to the back of the stretcher as the paramedics dashed Rick into the back of the waiting ambulance. Tubes and machinery followed the stretcher. Nancy ran out to the sidewalk, too, and watched as the ambulance pulled away from the curb, its siren wailing. Judd stood there, a worried expression on his face, his hands clenched into fists.

Nancy started to approach him, but a few of his team members got there first. She saw Judd scowl as one of the guys spoke to him. Then a few heated words were exchanged between Judd and a dark-haired runner.

What's going on? Nancy wondered. She waited until the guys had left, then she approached Judd.

"I'm sure he'll be okay," she said softly. "Has Rick ever had heart trouble before?"

"Not that I know of," Judd said, shaking his head.

"So what do you think happened to him?" Nancy asked.

"I don't know!" Judd burst out. "Why are you asking me?"

Nancy's mouth dropped open in surprise.

Immediately Judd apologized. "I'm really sorry, Nancy. It's just . . . never mind, I'm just really upset, that's all," he finished.

Nancy nodded and let the subject drop. But as she led him back inside to get their things, she couldn't help wondering why Judd had reacted like that. Was he keeping something from her?

It sure seemed that way. It made no sense that a well-conditioned athlete like Rick had collapsed on the dance floor.

CHAPTER 7

Stephanie felt delicious. It was Friday night, and she had draped herself on the sofa in Jonathan's living room. Her arms were stretched out across the back, her stockinged feet crossed on his rickety coffee table.

She surveyed the small room as if it were her newly conquered kingdom. It wasn't like her father's house with its ten bedrooms and king-size swimming pool. But it was hers. All hers.

Plus, Stephanie thought with satisfaction, they were starting out small—just the way her father always bragged that he had done. "With nothing but fifty bucks, a strong back, and a head full of dreams," he used to say. Now she couldn't wait to thrill him with the news about the big, responsible, adult step she was taking in her life.

"Stay right there," Jonathan called out from the kitchen. Stephanie heard a cork pop.

"Is this really happening?" she yelled over her shoulder toward the kitchen.

"I think so," Jonathan called back, sweeping into the room with two paper cups filled with champagne. He'd changed out of his work clothes and was wearing a striped sweater. "It feels like a dream, but we're really getting married."

"Mmmmmm," Stephanie said, taking the cup. "Thank you very, very much, Mr. Baur."

"You're welcome, Mrs. Baur."

Jonathan looked so excited and happy, Stephanie thought his smile was going to split his face in two as he raised his paper cup. "To you, Stephanie."

Stephanie shivered and took a sip. "Oh, Jonathan. I'm so happy."

Jonathan snuggled up close. "We going to have our own place together. And we're going to make big plans. And—well—you'll just always be able to count on me, Steph. I promise."

Stephanie gave him a sly smile and held out her clunky engagement ring. "Can I count on you to do something about this?"

"Sure," Jonathan promised, his smile faltering a little. "Sure, Steph. Just give me a little time. Okay?"

Stephanie drew him close and gave him a long kiss. "I know. Are you sure this is what you want?"

"Hey, my parents have been happily married for thirty years," Jonathan said. "And they tied the knot one month after meeting each other at the Illinois State Fair. They still live in the same little two bedroom house I grew up in, and they're happy as clams."

"Gee," Stephanie said.

"Wait until they meet you," Jonathan said proudly. "They won't believe my luck. They'll understand perfectly why I didn't wait."

Stephanie looked at him.

Jonathan sipped his champagne and smiled.

"Speaking of parents." Stephanie picked up the phone and held out the receiver. "Mind if I break the news to my dad while I'm here?"

Jonathan sprang up and poured himself another cup of champagne. "No. Go ahead. Tell him I can't wait to get together with him."

"Well, let's see what he says first," Stephanie said, punching in the phone number. On the outside, she was acting as if calling her father were the most casual act in the world. But inside, she was dreading it.

The last time she had really talked to her dad, he'd ended up canceling all but one of her credit cards. All because she hadn't flipped head over heels over Kiki. Well, now she'd give him a dose of his own medicine, Stephanie thought.

Stephanie braced herself inwardly.

"Hello?" came a high-pitched woman's voice on the phone.

"This is Stephanie Keats," Stephanie announced, completely ignoring the fact that it was Kiki on the other end of the line. "I want to speak to my father."

There was a pause. "Okay, Stephanie. Nice to hear your voice, too. I'll get him."

Stephanie made a face and stuck out her tongue at the receiver.

"Stephanie?" her father's voice boomed into the phone. "To what do we owe this honor?"

Stephanie grimaced. "Hello, Dad."

"Well, what is it?" her father wanted to know. "Good news? Trouble?"

"Good news," Stephanie said immediately, wrapping the telephone wire around her fingers and smiling. "Very good news."

"Yes?" her father muttered.

"I'm getting married," Stephanie blurted out.

"You're getting *what?*" her dad shouted into the phone.

"Married," Stephanie repeated. "I'm getting married to—"

"That's the craziest, stupidest idea I've ever heard in my life," Mr. Keats cut in.

Stephanie wrenched the receiver away from her ear so that she couldn't hear him.

". . . rushing into marriage like it's some kind of a game," her father was raving when she put the receiver back to her ear.

Stephanie felt her blood boil. "Oh, right," she cried out. "And you'd never rush into marriage?"

Out of the corner of her eye, she could see Jonathan's shocked expression.

"I'm a full-grown adult, able to take care of myself and provide for a family," her father returned. "And you are still a child."

Stephanie tossed her head. "Legally, I'm an adult, Dad. I can take care of myself."

"Your housing, food, and education are all being provided by me right now, Stephanie."

"I'm not a child and I'm not dependent on you."

"You certainly are, and you should thank your lucky stars for it. Who is this boy anyway?"

"His name is Jonathan Baur," Stephanie said indignantly.

"Jonathan Baur," her dad echoed. "How old is he?"

Stephanie drew herself up. "Jonathan is twenty-four. He's a college graduate and a manager with the Berrigan's Department Store in Weston."

There was a silence on the other end of the line. "Stephanie, honey," her dad began to plead. "Give it some thought."

"We're getting married on Wednesday," Stephanie said abruptly. "Why don't you come?"

"On Wed—" There was an audible sigh. "Stephanie. You're so young. Eighteen. You need to see a little more of the world first."

"I'm old enough, and I plan on seeing more of the world," Stephanie said angrily. "With Jonathan. We have big plans."

"And how are you going to carry out these grand plans on a department-store manager's salary, young lady?"

"He just got a raise," Stephanie said hotly.

"Well, don't expect a dime from me, Stephanie!" her father shouted into the phone. "I won't support this crazy plan of yours."

"Yeah?" Stephanie jeered back. "Well, that's fine with me."

"It won't be fine with you and your husband, young lady, when you no longer have R. J. Keats's money backing you," her father shouted.

"We don't want your money!" Stephanie yelled.

"You'll want it when your next tuition bill comes due," he warned.

"We can take care of ourselves!" Stephanie shouted.

"And don't expect me at the wedding," her father blared into the phone.

But Stephanie had already hung up on him.

"Park here," Nancy called out, pointing to an empty spot near the entrance to Weston General's emergency room.

Judd sped into the slot and jumped out of the car. "Come on."

Nancy hurried in through the emergency room's big automatic glass doors. Slipping through the crowded waiting room, they found a nurse behind the front counter.

"Rick Alexander," Judd called.

"He was brought in about twenty minutes ago," Nancy added.

The woman eyed Nancy and Judd. "They just took him to the intensive care unit on the second floor."

"Come on," Nancy said, grabbing Judd's arm.

When the elevator opened on the second floor, Nancy saw there was a spacious waiting room and a door to the intensive care unit at the far end. As they reached the door, however, they skidded to a stop.

"No Admittance," Judd said, reading the large red letters on the door. He tried to push it open, but it was locked.

Just then Nancy noticed another sign. "Use phone to contact nurses' station." She grabbed the phone. After a few rings someone answered.

"I'm Nancy Drew and I'm here with a close friend of Rick Alexander's," Nancy said calmly. "We're here to find out what his condition is."

"Are you a family member?" the nurse on the other end asked.

"No. He's a student at the university," she explained. "He has no family here in Weston."

"I'm sorry, Miss Drew," the nurse said curtly. "This is strict hospital policy. . . ."

Nancy was about to exchange words with the nurse when the doors to the ICU unit were flung open and Ginny burst in. She'd changed out of her tight jeans into sterile, head-to-toe surgical garb.

"Ginny," Nancy said, relieved. She hung up the phone. "Thank goodness you're here."

"Yeah, well, I heard the nurse on the phone with you. She's a real sweetheart, just following hospital procedure. I've done a lot of volunteer and training work with her, so she let me in."

"How is he?" Judd burst out.

"He's stable but unconscious," Ginny explained, looking worried. "And they don't know yet how much damage there is."

"You mean, he . . ." Judd faltered. "He might not make it?"

"It's hard to say," Ginny said seriously. "His doctors said that he'll need to regain consciousness within the next twenty-four to thirty-six hours."

"What do you mean by 'damage'?" Nancy wanted to know.

"Rick's heart muscle could have been severely damaged when it failed, because it lost oxygen," Ginny explained. "And then there could be brain damage, too."

"Brain damage?" Judd repeated. "This is a nightmare," he murmured.

"He's still on the ventilator," Ginny said. "I'm sorry to tell you this, Judd, but at this point it's really touch and go."

"Do they know what happened?" Nancy asked.

"They're doing some tests now," Ginny said. "He might have had some kind of congenital heart defect or even a bad virus."

"He had the flu a few weeks back," Judd said quietly, staring off into the distance.

Ginny moved closer. "Do you know if he was using any drugs, Judd? A lot of athletes can fall into that trap—steroids, amphetamines . . ."

"Rick wouldn't take any illegal drugs," Judd said.

Nancy narrowed her eyes. "It's so strange. He's an incredible runner. You'd think, if it were an illness, that it would have shown up earlier, on the track. Could it have been something he drank tonight or . . ."

"They'll find out," Judd said through clenched teeth. "I'm sure once the doctors look at him, they'll . . ."

His words trailed off as he spotted someone who'd just entered the waiting room. It was Coach Hayes. Judd hurried toward him.

"Nancy." Ginny grabbed her arm. "Heart problems can turn up in even the finest athletes. Sure, he didn't end up collapsing out on that track, but things were pretty wild at Club Z tonight."

"Yeah," Nancy agreed. "It just seems strange, doesn't it?"

"They're running a whole battery of tests on his blood and urine," Ginny explained. "Maybe something will turn up."

"Thanks, Gin," Nancy said, putting her hand on her shoulder. "You were amazing tonight."

"Nancy and Ginny?" Judd was saying behind her. "This is Chuck Hayes. Our coach."

"Hello," the coach said in a friendly manner.

Nancy stepped forward and shook the coach's hand. She recognized him immediately from the meet, though tonight he had on a sport coat and slacks.

"I came as soon as I heard the news," Coach Hayes said. "Judd tells me that you two took some pretty quick action at that club tonight. It sounds as though you saved Rick's life."

"He's still not out of the woods," Ginny reminded him. "But he's got some great doctors working on him."

Coach Hayes rubbed his forehead. "I just can't believe it. The kid's only eighteen."

Ginny nodded. "He's lucky to have such a supportive coach and teammates," she commented. "Not every coach would come to the hospital at this late hour."

Coach Hayes shook his head and waved off the compliment. "No problem. I just wanted to show my support. I'm going to be giving his family a call after I see him." He gave Ginny a slip of paper. "Here's their names and numbers. They'll be calling soon."

"Okay. Good," Ginny said quickly, taking the slip. "Gotta get back."

"Keep us posted on those test results, okay?" Nancy asked.

"I'll let you know as soon as I find out," Ginny replied, hurrying away.

"Hang in there, Judd," Coach Hayes said, putting his hand on Judd's shoulder. "Get some sleep. We'll talk tomorrow."

Judd's jaw muscles clenched. "Yeah. Okay."

"Need a ride back?" Coach Hayes asked.

"No—no," Judd answered, looking down. "Nancy's driving me home."

"Nice man," Nancy said as she watched the coach pick up the phone and talk to the nurse.

"Yeah," Judd said slowly. "And he was really pumped about Rick's future, especially after our last meet. He couldn't wait to work with him on his finishes. This afternoon, in fact . . ." His voice trailed off.

"In fact, what?" Nancy asked.

Judd shrugged as they headed for the elevator. "Oh nothing. Coach Hayes just worked him pretty hard this afternoon, that's all. I think Rick was tired."

"I bet he was," Nancy said, remembering how sweaty and shaky Rick had appeared after the meet. It seemed as though Rick Alexander always worked himself hard—very hard.

Just then the elevator came. As they got into the car, she couldn't help but notice the pain and confusion in Judd's blue eyes.

"Why were you so angry with your teammates after the ambulance took Rick away?" Nancy couldn't help asking.

Judd seemed to flinch at the question. "I'm just on edge. That's all, Nancy."

The doors closed, and they began their descent. Again Nancy had the uncomfortable feeling that Judd Wright was hiding something from her.

George knocked on Will's door the next morning.

After Rick Alexander had been taken away by paramedics, George had asked Will to drop her off at her dorm. Watching the runner nearly lose his life on the dance floor had really upset her. She hoped he was doing better this morning, but Ginny had reported that the situation was pretty grim.

Will came to the door in his sweats, sipping a mug of coffee.

"I thought you were going to run this morning," he said. He didn't smile. Both of them were still feeling the tension between them.

George bit her lip and walked in. A newspaper was spread over his kitchen table and the TV was on with the volume turned off.

"I thought I'd come to see you instead," George replied, sitting down.

"Oh."

George cleared her throat and stared at him. His shirt was rumpled and his long black hair fell around his face. Impulsively she stood up and gave him a kiss on the cheek.

"Physical contact?" he said, his voice laced with sarcasm. "I didn't know you were still interested."

George felt a pang. Will's eyes had a steely hardness that she'd never seen before.

George drew back from him. "Don't be sarcastic."

"How do you want me to be, George?"

George's face grew hot.

"What's going on with you?" Will went on angrily. "You don't want to dance close to me. You don't want to kiss me. And you definitely don't want to sleep with me."

"Don't you understand what I went through last week?" George demanded.

"I *know* what you went through," Will said gently, putting his large hand over hers. "You thought you were pregnant for a couple of days, and it was horrible for you. We've been over this a hundred times."

"It's still hard," George said.

"But it's over. We've got to move on," Will insisted. "It's getting a little—ridiculous."

"Ridiculous?" George repeated. The word stung. "Last week was ridiculous?"

"Well, maybe that was the wrong word," he said hastily. "The point is, you weren't pregnant, George. So forget about it."

"You really don't understand, do you?" George cried out. She stood up and paced across the room. "I'm using birth control, but no birth control is one hundred percent effective."

"Well, we'll just have to take that chance!" Will said, staring at her as if she were crazy.

"But I don't want to take that chance!" George heard herself say.

The apartment was totally silent.

"Is this some kind of indirect way of saying you don't want to be with me?" Will asked finally.

George closed her eyes in exasperation. "Let me get this straight. You think my worrying about getting pregnant is some kind of trick to get rid of you? You know what?" She shook her head. "You're not the center of the universe."

"Grow up, George," Will burst out. "You're being totally immature."

"You're wrong, Will. You're the one who needs to grow up. And I'm out of here."

"George," Will started. "Wait—"

But George didn't stop or even turn around. "It's over, Will," she yelled. She flung open his apartment door so hard that it banged back against the wall. "We're through." Then she took off as fast as she could.

CHAPTER 8

"This season's bridal look is decidedly sleek and formal, with a touch of the whimsical," Stephanie read in *American Bride* magazine. "Off-the-shoulder and backless styles work well, as long as they are filled out with generous floral additions, such as a cascading bouquet, or perhaps a full crown of roses or lilies of the valley holding the veil. . . ."

"Stephanie," a voice suddenly interrupted her thoughts.

Startled, Stephanie looked up. Nancy and Kara were standing in front of the couch in the lounge.

"Yoo-hoo," Kara teased, giving her bridal magazine a flick. "We know you're in paradise, but we need to get through to get hot water for tea."

Stephanie drew up her legs so they could pass. It was true, planning her wedding *was* like being in paradise.

88

"What are you doing up so early?" Kara asked, bobbing her tea bag up and down in her mug.

Stephanie looked up. "And what are you doing? Experimenting with a twig-and-bark tea this morning?"

"This happens to be a very good jasmine tea," Kara said good-naturedly, flopping down on a chair. "Come on. Tell us why you're out of bed before noontime on a weekend."

Stephanie flipped back a strand of her long hair. "Jonathan had to get on the floor early this morning. Big weekend sale in home and appliances. So I came back here."

Nancy got her tea, then sat down with a wide yawn. "We're still trying to wake up," she said.

"Stayed up too late at Club Z, huh?" Stephanie said. "Dawn told me about that guy collapsing on the dance floor," she went on. "That's so weird. Was he doing drugs or anything?"

"I heard he's a straight-arrow athlete," Kara said.

Stephanie shrugged. "Lots of those clean-cut athletes take steroids, you know. They'll do anything to win."

Abruptly Nancy changed the subject. "Making wedding plans?"

"Sure am," Stephanie replied. "Wednesday is going to be the most important day of my life. I want it to be perfect."

The girls listened to her talk about her plans for a few more minutes. Then Kara stood up.

"Bye, guys," Kara said, wrapping her hands around her teacup. "I'm going to take a shower before I hit the books."

As Kara left, Stephanie flashed Nancy a grateful smile. "Can you believe this is happening?"

Nancy hesitated. "It's pretty exciting," she admitted. "But . . ."

"What?" Stephanie demanded.

"Have you guys considered giving things more time?" Nancy asked her.

Stephanie felt a spark of anger. "You were the one who suggested that I make a commitment, Nancy," she snapped. "Now that I've done that, I can't believe I don't have your support."

Nancy's mouth dropped open. "Oh, Stephanie. Marriage isn't the kind of commitment I was talking about—at least not right away."

Stephanie glared as Nancy went on. "If you love Jonathan and want to make a commitment, then take your time," Nancy continued. "Get yourselves ready for this. This is the biggest decision you'll ever make in your life."

Nancy Drew didn't understand her feelings toward Jonathan at all. "I know what I'm doing," Stephanie said coldly. "And I'm ready for it. But thanks for the input," she added sarcastically.

Nancy was quiet for a moment. "Okay, Steph," she said, standing up. "It sounds like you are ready. Let me know if you need any help," she added on her way out.

Stephanie fumed as she watched Nancy leave.

Just like her dad, Nancy was treating her like a big baby.

"Nobody wants to support me and Jonathan on this," she mumbled. Just when she needed her friends, they were letting her down.

"Don't say a word to her about waiting longer," Nancy said once she was back in her room with Kara. "She doesn't want to hear it."

"I could wring her skinny, little pampered neck," Kara said. "Why is she so determined to get married all of a sudden?"

Nancy shrugged. Before she could reply, Eileen O'Connor burst into the room. "You're not going to believe this!"

"What's wrong?" Nancy stood up. Eileen's face looked white beneath her freckles.

Eileen sank down on Nancy's bed. "After you and Judd left for the hospital last night, the police came to Club Z."

"Why?" Kara asked.

"Because Rick collapsed at the club," Eileen said worriedly, "I think they suspect drugs."

"His friends swear he doesn't use them," Nancy said.

"Maybe his teammates are protecting him," Eileen said. "He could have had some kind of overdose."

Kara nodded.

"If the cops wanted to, they could shut down Club Z and destroy Jason's business," Eileen said. "They questioned him until about two in the morning."

"Look," Nancy said, patting Eileen on the shoulder. "Ginny Yuen's going to call after she gets Rick's blood and urine test results. If they don't find any trace of drugs, then Jason won't have anything to worry about."

Eileen nodded but she was still upset.

Just then there was a quiet knock on the door. It was Ginny. Her black hair was slipping out of a ponytail and she looked exhausted.

"I checked on Rick a while ago. He's still stable," Ginny said, rubbing her eyes and sitting down on Nancy's desk chair. "But he's not off the ventilator. He still can't breathe by himself."

"Boy, that sounds really serious," Eileen whispered.

"Yeah," Ginny said. "Heart failure *is* serious."

Nancy shook her head. "Then there's a good chance that Rick can never run again—at least not at the same incredible times."

Ginny nodded. "Right."

"Have they finished running tests on him?" Nancy asked.

"So far, the EKG and the echocardiogram don't show any heart defect," Ginny said. "And they haven't found any traces of hard drugs, steroids, or alcohol."

"Thank goodness!" Eileen exclaimed.

"Judd said Rick had the flu a couple of weeks ago," Nancy thought out loud. "He might have checked into the university health center."

Ginny nodded. "It's possible."

"Maybe we could get the hospital to request copies of those records?" Nancy suggested. "Maybe it wasn't the flu. Maybe it was something else."

"Whew!" Pam exclaimed, slowing to a jog. "What's gotten into you, George? You're running as if you've got fire under your feet."

"What's that?" George panted. "Four miles or five?"

"Five," Pam said, stopping and holding on to her side. "Five times around the lake."

"Oh," George said absently. She stopped running and bent over, to stretch out her muscles.

Suddenly it hit her. It was Saturday night, almost the first Saturday night since college began that she had spent without Will.

"George?" Pam said as she sat down and grabbed her feet. "You seem awfully distracted."

"Will and I broke up this morning," George said quietly. "At least I think we did."

"What?" Pam exclaimed, sitting straight up. "What happened?"

George felt a lump in her throat. "He—he just didn't understand, Pam."

"Oh," Pam said, looking down. "You mean, about last week?"

George nodded. "After I found out I wasn't pregnant, he wanted to go on as if nothing had happened. But for me . . ." Her voice trailed off. "It changed everything."

"Yeah, I bet it made you think twice about what you guys have been doing," Pam said softly.

"I wish it had made Will think, too," George said. "He just wants to jump right back into bed, as if nothing happened."

"It's different for guys," Pam said. "We're the ones who get pregnant so we're forced to take more responsibility."

George nodded. "I've realized that there are real consequences to having sex. Some pretty scary ones. And I can't handle them now."

Pam was quiet, waiting for George to continue.

"Will thinks I'm being childish. But maybe that's the point. I *am* too young to be in a relationship that feels so grown up."

Pam reached over and hugged her. "Maybe he'll come around," she said softly. "Will's a great guy, George."

"Maybe he will come around," George said with a sigh. "And maybe he won't. In the meantime, my two best friends still aren't speaking to each other. I have no idea what to do about that problem either."

"Now, that's something I *know* will work out over time," Pam said. "Nancy and Bess have been friends for ages. They've worked out problems before."

"Not like this one," George said doubtfully. "I'm starting to think they'll never patch things up. Men," she grumbled. "They mess up everything."

Pam grinned. "Is that what they said at a Sekhmet Society meeting?"

"Sort of," George admitted. "I'm only half joking about men," she went on. "If Ned had stayed away from Bess in the first place, the whole thing would never have happened."

Pam shrugged. "You can't blame him for being supportive of Bess after Paul died. The real problem is that Bess and Nancy haven't talked yet," she went on.

"That's true," George agreed as she and Pam started back toward their room. "There's got to be some way to make them work it out."

"Hey!" Suddenly Pam stopped and grabbed George by her shoulders. "I've got it."

"You've got what?" George said.

"An idea. It's sort of an old trick," Pam went on. "But you know what? It just might work."

Nancy checked her watch as she hurried back to Thayer Hall after a quick Saturday night dinner at the Cave with Kara.

"Your message machine is blinking," Kara said as they entered their room. "Maybe it's Judd with an update on Rick."

Eagerly, Nancy hit the Rewind button.

"Hi, Nancy," came Judd's hoarse voice from the machine. "I'm back now. Give me a call when you can."

Nancy dug his number out of her backpack and quickly punched it into the phone.

"Hello?" Judd answered. His voice sounded tired and far away.

"It's Nancy. Are you okay? I've been trying to reach you."

"Yeah," Judd replied. He cleared his throat. "Yeah. I'm okay. I've just been stuck at the athletic center all day."

Nancy sensed something was wrong. "What's up?"

There was a long sigh. "I went for a short workout late this morning, and some officer from the Weston Police Department tracked me down."

"They were questioning Jason Lehman down at Club Z, too," Nancy told him as she sat back on a pillow. "I guess they're checking to see if Rick had been taking drugs."

There was a pause on the other end of the line. "Yeah."

"Did they ask you about drugs, too?"

"Yes," Judd replied, his voice quiet. "They asked me about drugs and if there was anything suspicious about Rick's personal life. Stuff like that."

"Do you need to talk?" Nancy asked. "You sound pretty upset."

There was a long pause. "No, Nancy. I can't talk right now. But thanks, anyway. Look," he went on abruptly. "I'll give you a call when I know something more about Rick."

As he hung up, Nancy pressed her lips. What was going on with Judd? One day he was asking her out, and the next day he seemed to be dissing her or something.

She doubted that either Judd or Rick were into drugs. So why was he acting so guarded?

Nancy grabbed her backpack. "Thanks for dinner, Kara," she said. "If anyone needs me, I'll be down at the news room."

Kara made a face. "On a Saturday night?"

Nancy nodded. She had no idea what she was looking for, but her instincts told her there was something to be found.

"Hi, guys," Nancy called across the *Times* news room. The sports desk was in its usual Saturday-night disarray—covered with empty pizza boxes, pages of marked-up copy, and Norsemen team schedules. The sound of furious typing was nearly drowned out by blaring rock music.

"Hi, Gail." Nancy poked her head into Gail Gardeski's cubicle. She was running through a menu of that week's stories on her computer.

"Hey." Gail pushed her chair back and looked up at Nancy with interest. "That men's cross-country story has a new angle, huh? I heard about that kid collapsing down at Club Z last night."

Nancy nodded. "He's in serious condition still."

"Stay on top of the story," Gail told her. "It'll generate a lot of interest in the paper."

As Nancy headed for her cubicle, she bumped into Jake Collins, another reporter with the *Times*. Nancy and Jake had dated for a while. As always, Jake was wearing his jeans and cowboy boots. He was concerned about Rick, too. "Do you think that freshman was doing drugs?" he asked.

"I don't know," Nancy admitted. "But I met him before it happened and he seems like a nice kid."

Jake nodded and put a hand on Nancy's shoulder before turning away. "Let me know if you need any help with the story." She thanked him, then continued on her way to her cubicle, where her computer screen saver danced green and blue in the darkness. Everyone kept asking if Rick had been doing drugs. It was obviously on everyone's mind.

"So let's do a little background research on Wilder's newly famous men's cross-country team," she muttered to herself, punching her keyboard.

"Got it," Nancy said a few moments later. She scanned the story, which had been written at the beginning of the school year. The headline was "Winning St. Vincent's University Coach Snagged by Wilder."

"St. Vincent's," Nancy muttered to herself. "That's a top school in cross-country. Very impressive." Nancy read on.

After turning St. Vincent's formerly lackluster men's cross-country program into an NCAA contender and sending its top runner to the Olympic trials, Coach Chuck Hayes says he wants to get back to his hometown roots in Weston.

"It's good to be back," Coach Hayes told the *Wilder Times*. "I look forward to spending more time with my parents, who've had several medical emergencies in the past year."

Nancy scanned the rest of the story. Coach Hayes was clearly a very likable guy. Wilder had been lucky to get him away from a prestigious school like St. Vincent's.

"Okay—now," Nancy muttered, her fingers flying over the keyboard in the dim light. "What else have we got?"

She spotted an article the *Times* sports department had written just a few days before she'd taken over the story. "Plummeting Times on Wilder Cross-Country Send Hopes Soaring."

"Mmmm." She scanned the article.

Last year the Norsemen finished last in all meets and nearly all events. This year the team may finish first in its conference. Veterans Rudy Milton, Lance Macon, and Brett Gold showed the most impressive gains.

Nancy sat back in her chair and stared at the screen. Coach Hayes was truly doing an impressive job.

Nancy reached for a pen and jotted down the names of the three runners who'd improved their times most dramatically: Rudy Milton, Lance Macon, and Brett Gold. She wanted to interview these guys.

Even if they couldn't tell her more about Rick Alexander, maybe they could help her learn more about the secret to Coach Hayes's amazing success.

CHAPTER 9

Reluctantly, Bess opened her eyes. The pale morning sunlight was filtering in through the window over her bed.

Relief flooded over her as she remembered that it was Sunday morning. Good. She didn't have to get up and face the day or biology or her problems with Nancy and Ned.

"There's a note for you, Bess," Leslie said suddenly. "Are you awake?"

"A note?" Bess mumbled. She sat up. There was Leslie, standing over her like a freshly ironed reminder of how bad she felt.

"Yeah," Leslie said. "Here. Someone slipped it under the door."

Bess took the pink envelope, then turned it over.

"Bess" was printed neatly on the front. As she tore it open, she felt her heart climb into her throat. It was handwriting she knew well.

Dear Bess,

I'm so sorry about everything. I know I overreacted when I saw you and Ned saying goodbye. Your friendship is very important to me. Can you meet me for breakfast this morning at the Bumblebee Diner? I'll be there at ten o'clock.

Fondly,
Nancy

As Bess reread the letter, she felt an enormous weight lifting. "Oh my gosh," she murmured. "Nancy's not angry anymore."

The fight with her best friend was over. Bess sprang out of bed and grabbed her shower things. Breakfast with Nancy at the Bumblebee Diner. She couldn't wait to see her!

No one in the Thayer Hall third-floor suite was stirring. The coffee machine was cold. The showers were silent. Not even an MTV special had been turned on on the television. So no one heard the *ding* of the elevator and the footsteps heading for Nancy's door.

"Hey," Kara said in a sleepy voice a few minutes later. "There's some kind of note on the floor."

Nancy just groaned and rolled over. She'd stayed at the news room, working on her article, until after midnight.

"It's for you," Kara said, scooping up the envelope.

Nancy heard her roommate padding across the floor. Then she felt her place the envelope in her hand.

"A message slipped under the door," Kara whispered excitedly. "How mysterious."

Nancy finally lifted her head, then looked at the note in her hand. When she saw the familiar handwriting, she ripped open the flap.

Dear Nan,

I'm really sorry about what has happened between us. Please try to understand that Ned is a friend and nothing more. It was just a hug, Nan. Your friendship is important to me. Meet me at the Bumblebee at ten o'clock this morning. We'll talk then.

Fondly,
Bess

Nancy reread the note. You totally jumped to conclusions about Bess and Ned! she chided herself. And she'd been doubly wrong not to give Bess a chance to explain. She'd been stupid, childish, and unfair.

"I should be the one apologizing, Bess," Nancy whispered to herself.

A moment later Nancy was out of bed and heading for the showers, wide-awake and feeling better than she had all week. After watching Rick nearly die on the dance floor, she'd been reminded of how fleeting life can be—and how precious her friends were to her.

She couldn't wait to get to the Bumblebee.

"Keep your head down," George said in a hushed voice.

Pam giggled and took another bite of her Bumblewaffle. "How much longer?"

George slid down farther in the vinyl seat at the back of the diner. "They should be arriving any minute now."

"I hope our plan works," Pam said under her breath.

"It will," George said with certainty.

But inside, she had her doubts. Meddling in this conflict between Nancy and Bess might only make things worse. What would happen when the two of them realized that someone else had written the notes?

"Check it out." Pam nodded in the direction of the door. "It looks like half the Wilder University men's cross-country team is coming in to eat breakfast. And are they in great shape."

George grinned. "What if Jamal heard you, Pam!" Jamal Lewis was Pam's boyfriend.

"So?" Pam grinned back. "A girl can look, can't she?"

"Here's Nancy," George said a second later. "She's pulling up right in front of the door."

"Here goes," Pam said.

"Now she's walking in the door," George whispered, slipping down even farther in her back booth seat. "She's looking around. Oh, here comes Bess right behind her. Okay, they're smiling at each other!"

"And now—they're hugging!" Pam chimed in happily. "This is so great."

"I know," George joined in. Triumphantly, the roommates exchanged high-fives. But George's high spirits crashed a moment later when she saw Bess shake her head. With a confused expression, Nancy reached into her backpack and drew out a pink envelope.

By this time Bess was digging into her backpack, too. George watched in horror as Bess pulled out the pink envelope and said something to Nancy, her eyes flashing angrily.

"What's going on, Nancy?" Bess demanded, crumpling the pink envelope in her hand. "Is this some kind of a joke? You didn't write this apology?"

Nancy's face was turning red. "No."

"Well, then, who did?" Bess demanded.

"I don't know." Nancy looked uncomfortable. "Let's sit down."

Bess stomped over to the nearest booth. To her surprise, she suddenly felt furious—as if all her pent-up feelings had suddenly boiled up. "Well, you *should* have written it," she snapped.

Nancy's jaw dropped. "*I* should have written it? *You* should have written me an apology! How do you think I felt standing there in your doorway, staring at you and Ned—"

"I'm the one who's been trying to talk to you, Nancy," Bess interrupted her. She crossed her arms over her chest and glared. "You've been doing everything you can to avoid me."

Nancy was silent as Bess's words sunk in. "I should have listened," she murmured. "But I—I just couldn't."

Bess felt herself soften. "In all of the years I've known you, Nancy," she said softly, "I've never seen you so stubborn."

"I've never suspected that my best friend was involved with my boyfriend," Nancy blurted out.

"Your *ex*-boyfriend," Bess said pointedly. "And what do I have to give you to convince you that we're just friends? A signed legal document swearing that we've never kissed?"

"Yes," Nancy said solemnly.

Bess just sat there, stunned. "What?"

"And witnessed by a notary," Nancy added. A tiny smile formed on her stony face.

Bess narrowed her eyes.

"And I want it signed in blood," Nancy went on.

That was all Bess needed. She burst into laughter.

Nancy was laughing now, too. In fact, she was laughing so hard that she dropped her face into her arms, which were folded on the table.

"We've been acting really crazy," Bess said.

"I know," Nancy said. It was true. They *had* been acting crazy.

All because you haven't gotten over Ned Nickerson, came a voice from inside.

"I've missed you, Nan," Bess was saying.

Nancy took her friend's hand. "How could we have let this happen?"

"I don't know, Nan. But I'm so sorry. And I'm so grateful that this note came—"

Suddenly Bess stopped talking.

"The pink envelopes!" she and Nancy said in unison as they looked around the room.

All at once they noticed George standing there.

"I'm sorry. I just had to do it," she said, slipping into the booth next to Nancy. Pam was with her.

"I didn't have anything to do with this." Pam grinned as she dropped down next to Bess. "I just came along for the Bumblewaffle."

"I could have sworn that was Nancy's handwriting," Bess admitted. "How did you do it?"

George shrugged. "I've been looking at her handwriting for years. I know it by heart. Yours, too," she added, looking at her cousin.

Bess squeezed George's hand. "Thanks."

"We have to stick together," George said simply. "We can't let men tear us apart. Okay?"

Nancy took George's hand, a little surprised by her friend's choice of words. "I think your women's group is helping us all," she said, smiling.

"Speaking of men and women," Pam spoke up. "Check out the team's order."

"Whoa! That's some serious food!" Bess

watched the waitress unload plates heaped with eggs and bacon and waffles. "Those guys are eating enough for twelve."

"They're runners. They'll burn it off," George said.

Pam caught Nancy peering at the group of guys.

"Hey, Nancy," she said slyly, "I heard about your date with Judd Wright."

Bess looked at Nancy. "So, do you like him, Nan?"

As Nancy smiled back at her, Bess felt a surge of warmth for her old friend. It seemed as if they'd been apart forever, and there was so much to catch up on.

"I do like him, Bess," Nancy said wistfully. "But—I just can't get involved with anyone right now. I'm not ready."

"Good for you, Nancy," George chimed in. "I think it's really important for women to make decisions based on what's best for them."

Nancy nodded thoughtfully for a minute. "I'm surprised Judd isn't with his buddies. Maybe he's over at the hospital, checking on Rick Alexander."

Everyone leaned forward.

"How is he, Nan?" Bess asked.

"I heard he has something wrong with his heart," George said.

Nancy shook her head. "A heart defect has been ruled out by his doctors. They're still doing tests to figure out why he collapsed."

"What about drugs?" Bess asked. "Was he on steroids or amphetamines or anything?"

Nancy shrugged. "That seems to be the question on everyone's mind."

"Weird," George said, shaking her head.

"It sure makes me appreciate the time I spend with my friends," Bess said.

Nancy gave Bess a big smile. "I know exactly what you mean."

After the girls had finished breakfast, Nancy slipped out of the booth at the diner and fished in her pocket for change to leave a tip for the waitress.

"Hey, Nancy," came a male voice suddenly.

Nancy turned to look. A second group of Judd's friends from the team had come into the diner. One of them was gesturing to her. "Come here for a second," said a tall guy with freckles. His hair was still wet from his morning workout.

When Nancy went over, he introduced himself as Lance Macon. "We met down at Club Z Friday night before, uh . . ." he faltered.

"Oh, yes. I remember," Nancy said. Judd had introduced the two of them before Rick's collapse.

"This is Rudy Milton, Brett Gold, and Steve Goltz." Lance gestured around the table. There were a few brief nods and uncomfortable looks. Lance cleared his throat as Nancy said hello. These were the guys she'd been hoping to interview.

"Look," Lance said. "I—we—just wanted to say thanks for helping Rick on Friday night. You and that premed student saved his life."

"That was Ginny Yuen," Nancy said.

"Right," Lance said, tapping his head as if he'd forgotten her name. "She sure knows how to think on her feet."

The other guys in the booth shifted in their seats. *What's going on with these guys?* Nancy wondered. They must have had a reason for calling her over, and she was willing to bet it wasn't to make small talk.

"Judd says you're writing an article about the team for the *Times,*" the guy named Rudy said. He had thin dark hair, pale skin, and very broad shoulders that shifted nervously when he spoke. He took a big swig of his orange juice as he looked her straight in the eye.

"Yes," Nancy said, staring back at him. "I am."

"Are you going to write about Rick?" Lance asked.

"That will be part of my story," Nancy replied carefully. "A lot of people want to know what happened. I was actually hoping to interview a few of you guys to get your thoughts."

Rudy set down his glass and glared at her.

Nancy saw Lance and Brett exchange a glance before Lance said, "Most of us are on scholarships, including Judd. Negative publicity in the paper could do damage to our careers, you know."

"What do you mean by negative publicity?" Nancy asked.

"There's talk all over campus about steroids," Rudy jumped in, "as well as lots of other crazy rumors about the team that aren't true."

"I'm not sure why you're so concerned about my story," Nancy said evenly. "As far as I know, no one has accused the team of anything." She let her words hang in the air for a minute. "The *Times* doesn't print gossip," she went on. "So you can be sure that I'll write truthfully about any information I get on Rick's health problems. Even if it doesn't reflect well on the team," she added.

The runners just stared at her for a minute.

Then Rudy narrowed his eyes. "You write your article," he said quietly. "But if it does anything to tarnish our reputations, you'll be hearing from us."

CHAPTER 10

The Fleur du Jour flower shop was located in downtown Weston, just off a lovely brick plaza lined with upscale dress shops, restaurants, and hair salons.

Stephanie pushed open the door and breathed in the delicious steamy fragrance of the shop. A refrigerated glass case held bushels of red, pink, and yellow roses in big plastic tubs. Nestled close to them were bunches of purple gladiolas, white snapdragons, and spiky yellow mums.

Stephanie took in the pots of delicate white cyclamen tied with huge pink bows. The potted rose trees and ivy topiaries. A white arch with indoor orange blossoms creeping up its side.

"May I help you?" a guy with shaggy blond hair asked her. In his silk Hawaiian shirt, he looked as if he'd just returned from the tropics.

"Yes," Stephanie said. "I need to order some flowers."

111

"Is it a special occasion?" he asked, skimming her body with his eyes.

A shiver traveled up her spine. This guy had the most intense aquamarine eyes. "Uh—yes," Stephanie said. In the nick of time, a voice inside reminded her not to flirt. "I'm getting married on Wednesday," she said firmly.

"Married?" The guy's face fell. "Mmmm, sorry to hear that," he said under his breath.

"It's going to be an indoor ceremony," Stephanie said in a businesslike tone. Even though a part of her was disappointed about not trying to get to know this guy, another part of her was very pleased. Her idea to make a commitment and get married was already working like a charm. She had stopped herself from flirting with this very cute man. "At least I think it's going to be indoors. My colors will be pink and white," she added.

"Okay," the clerk said. "Let's take a look at our wedding book and do a little brainstorming."

"Let's start with the bride's bouquet," Stephanie suggested.

She was eager to put together something really special for herself, since the wedding dress Jonathan had helped her pick out at Berrigan's wasn't the most elaborate or beautiful dress she'd seen on the rack. Stephanie had wanted something a bit nicer from a better-known designer, but since she had to rely on Jonathan's employee credit card to buy it, there wasn't much she could do.

And Jonathan had been firm about keeping the cost down.

The only practical solution, Stephanie decided, was to splurge on flowers. After all, she was only planning to get married once.

What's more, how much could flowers cost? She didn't really know, since she had never bought flowers for anyone. Anyway, she had Jonathan's credit card firmly in hand, and she would be ready to use it when the moment came.

"I want a very large rose bridal bouquet," Stephanie explained. "And then I want everything else to coordinate with that."

"Yes," the clerk said, his face thoughtful. "We have some nice potted roses. You could use these to bank up against the altar. Are you being married in a church?"

"Well, I don't know," Stephanie faltered. "I mean, no, not a church."

The guy looked confused.

"We're still working out the last-minute details," Stephanie said with finality, striding toward an elaborate arrangement of delicate white blossoms. "I like this."

"Oh, yes," the guy said. "The owner just brought these rare orchids over from Hawaii in a refrigerated container. They grow in a private rain forest on the island of Kauai."

"Fine," Stephanie said briskly. "I'll take two of these arrangements."

The guy began scribbling eagerly on an order form. "The full-length pink and white rose bridal bouquet, ten pots of miniature roses, and two of the large orchid display arrangements."

"Yes," Stephanie agreed, proudly slipping Jonathan's gold credit card on the counter. If her father could only see her now, Stephanie thought with satisfaction. He thought she was still a child, but she'd managed to make all these arrangements completely on her own.

"Thank you very much for your order," the guy said a moment later. "I hope you have a beautiful and happy ceremony."

"I'll let you know by Tuesday where to deliver them," Stephanie said with great dignity. As she signed the bill with a flourish, she paid absolutely no attention to the amount she'd charged on Jonathan's card.

"Ginny? Has Judd been over at the hospital checking on Rick?" Nancy asked. She was in a library phone booth, where she'd already dialed Judd's dorm room and the paging service at the student union.

Finally she'd managed to track down Ginny, who was volunteering in the hospital's pediatrics wing all afternoon.

"Yes," Ginny confirmed. "I ran into him in the hospital parking lot as he was leaving. Rick's still unconscious, and Judd's pretty upset about it."

Nancy frowned. "I ran into a few of his teammates at the Bumblebee this morning. They were acting so weird, Gin. I've got to talk to Judd about what's going on with the team."

"Maybe they're all feeling defensive," Ginny suggested. "There's a lot of gossip going around campus about what made Rick's heart fail."

"I know that most of it is gossip," Nancy said. "But I still think the team members are hiding something."

"Rick's drug tests came back negative, Nancy," Ginny reminded her. "There was no trace of alcohol, steroids, amphetamines, or other hard drugs."

"Yeah, I know." Nancy sighed. "The whole thing is very strange. I think I'll try to find Judd at the athletic center."

"Okay," Ginny said. "Don't forget that Casey Fontaine wants us to meet her at Java Joe's in an hour. I think it has something to do with Stephanie's wedding."

"Speaking of strange events . . ." Nancy murmured.

Ginny chuckled. "I'll see you later, Nan."

Nancy put down the phone and checked her watch. Then she hurried out the library's main entrance into the tree-lined quad. From there she jogged down to the athletic center at the edge of campus, dodging students.

Inside the center, Nancy made her way down two flights of stairs to the basement, where the team's locker room was. On her right was a long concrete hallway leading to the locker rooms. On her left was a door that led to the team's outdoor training field. Nancy opened the door. Outside she spotted Judd, Rudy, Lance, and the others working with Coach Hayes. They were deep in concentration and didn't notice her.

Nancy hesitated for a second, then let the door close. With all of the members of the team busy outside, it suddenly seemed like the perfect time to do some investigating.

Cautiously, Nancy headed back toward the men's locker room. She stood quietly for a second, listening for the sound of a banging locker or running water.

She pushed the door open partway. "Hello?"

Satisfied that the room was empty, Nancy stepped inside. A row of black lockers lined one wall, and discarded warm-up pants, sweaty T-shirts, and running shoes were scattered all over.

Nancy scanned the room, uncertain what she was looking for.

Then she spotted a gym bag under a bench. The words *Wilder Cross-country* were stitched next to the top zipper.

Nancy started for the bag.

"Brett!" A guy's voice right outside the door startled her. Nancy darted behind a wall of lockers as the door was opened. "You in here?" someone yelled.

A moment later Nancy heard the door close and then the footsteps head off down the hall. "Whew," she muttered to herself. "That was close." As Nancy stepped out of her hiding spot, her eyes landed again on the gym bag. This time she noticed the initials *RM* embroidered on the side of the bag.

RM—Rudy Milton, she guessed. Impulsively, she hurried over to the bag and undid the zipper.

"Come on, come on," Nancy whispered to herself, carefully watching the door as she sorted through the bag's contents: a pair of socks, hairbrush, deodorant, towel, a shaving kit. Suddenly her fingertips brushed against an inside pouch. Quickly she reached inside.

Nancy's eyes widened as she pulled out a small plastic bag containing a dozen or so large white tablets. Before Nancy could examine the pills more closely, voices echoed down the hallway.

Her heart in her throat, Nancy opened the bag and slipped out one tablet. Then she stuck the bag back inside the zippered pocket and darted toward the back of the locker room.

Nancy looked around in a panic as the voices of the runners drew nearer. Where on earth was she going to hide? A split second later she spotted an Exit sign across the room.

Without another thought, Nancy dashed for the door, and pushed it open. Relief flooded through her as she found herself in broad daylight in a secluded alley that ran alongside the building.

"So you don't do drugs, huh, guys," Nancy murmured, pulling the tablet out of her pocket and looking at it again.

She headed for Java Joe's to meet her friends,

wondering if she had just found what the team was trying so hard to hide.

"Oh, good, you're here," Casey Fontaine said as Nancy entered the coffee shop. Casey sat at the head of a table. A long notepad, filled with lists and studded with Post-it notes, was in front of her.

Nancy sat down and looked around in surprise. Practically everyone from Thayer Hall Suite 301 was there: Ginny, Dawn, Eileen, Kara, Liz, and Reva.

Nancy collapsed in her chair, still shaking from her ordeal inside the men's locker room. Nervously, she fingered the small tablet inside her pocket.

"Okay, let's get this meeting under way," Casey announced. She was wearing a funky polka-dot top and Planet Hollywood earrings, but her face was all business. "As you know, Stephanie Keats has been my roommate almost since the beginning of the semester . . ."

There was a round of applause, peppered with a few hollers of support.

Casey stood up and bowed. "Okay. Okay. I know that Stephanie hasn't been—well, the *perfect* roommate."

Kara was shaking her head. "You can say that again."

Casey held up one finger. "However, she *is* my roommate, and she's trying very hard right now to settle down."

Everyone nodded.

"Stephanie is planning to marry Jonathan three days from now, on Wednesday," Casey reminded everyone. "It hasn't exactly been the longest engagement in the history of Western civilization."

A few giggles erupted.

"Still," Casey went on, "Stephanie's determined to do this. And I want to give her support—as a friend."

"But, Casey," Liz objected, "this plan of Stephanie's is just a—"

"What I'm proposing," Casey interrupted her in a loud voice, "is a surprise shower. In our suite. Monday night. That's tomorrow, folks."

"Pots and pans and blenders for Stephanie?" Liz cracked. "She'd laugh in our faces."

"No," Casey explained. "I'm proposing a lingerie shower."

"Now, *that's* right up Stephanie's alley," Dawn said, grinning.

Casey nodded. "We won't have to spend a fortune either. I'm thinking slippers, bubble bath, underwear. Maybe a few of us can go in on a pretty nightgown."

"I'm for it," Nancy said enthusiastically. She still wasn't sure that Stephanie's marriage was such a good idea, but she admired Casey's loyalty to her roommate.

"Great," Casey said, checking something off on her pad. "Now—one more important detail. Stephanie doesn't have a clue where they can get married in this town."

"She doesn't?" Ginny gasped. "The wedding is only three days away!"

Casey sighed. "She's called a few nice places, but of course they need far more notice."

Nancy shook her head. What was Stephanie thinking?

"So I've talked the Kappas into letting Stephanie have her wedding ceremony and reception at our house on Wednesday night," Casey explained.

Nancy smiled. Casey belonged to the Kappa sorority, whose off-campus house was large and beautiful.

"You are a saint," Liz muttered.

"Yeah, well, it took some convincing Soozie and Holly," Casey admitted. "But here's the deal: the Kappas want something in exchange. They want our entire suite to volunteer hours for the next charity event. What do you say?"

"Sure," Dawn said.

Nancy looked up. All around the table her friends were nodding. No matter how difficult Stephanie had been in the past, everyone was ready and eager to pitch in to make her wedding day a happy occasion.

Casey grinned. "Great. Then it's settled. Really appreciate it, you guys." She waved a paper in the air. "Here's a gift sign-up sheet."

After the group had broken up, Nancy grabbed Ginny. "I need to show you something," she said in a low voice.

"What is it?" Ginny asked, sweeping back her silky black hair as she slung her backpack over a shoulder. Nancy walked with her out into the afternoon sun.

"I found this," Nancy said, pulling the tablet out of her pocket.

"Where?" Ginny asked curiously.

Nancy hesitated. "In a gym bag belonging to someone on the men's team."

Ginny stopped walking. "Nancy . . ." she said warningly.

"I know," Nancy said, putting the tablet in Ginny's palm. "But it was for a good cause. Do you know anyone at the hospital who can analyze this?"

Ginny nodded. "Alison Watters. She's a friend of mine—one of the pharmacists down at the lab. I bet she'd run some tests for me."

"Thanks, Ginny," Nancy said. "I'd really like to get to the bottom of this situation with Rick."

"I've actually got good news regarding Rick," Ginny said.

"What?" Nancy grabbed her friend's arm.

"He's regained consciousness," Ginny said. "It happened right after you called me this afternoon. By the time I left the hospital, they'd taken him off the ventilator and his responses were looking good. So the worst is over."

"That's great," Nancy said.

"Yeah, and another thing," Ginny said, looking at Nancy. "I was able to talk to the doctors about his blood and urine tests."

Nancy swallowed hard. "Drugs?" she asked.

Ginny shook her head. "A virus. He had some kind of acute virus that got into his heart."

"It actually caused his heart to fail?" Nancy asked.

"It's called viral cardiomyopathy," Ginny explained. "It weakened his heart and caused it to start going into an arrhythmia—an irregular heartbeat. The doctors aren't quite sure why his heart completely failed on him. But it sometimes happens. Do you still want me to have this tablet analyzed?"

Nancy thought for a second. "Maybe I'm crazy, Ginny. But I can't shake the feeling that something suspicious is going on. I mean, why does everyone on the team seem so afraid of my news story? It's as if they're worried I'll discover something about Rick's collapse."

"So you *do* want me to have it checked out—right?" Ginny said.

Nancy nodded. "I'll check with you later—okay?" Holding the pill, Ginny hurried away.

Nancy locked her car and hurried across the crowded parking lot to Weston General Hospital.

"I'm looking for Ginny Yuen," Nancy explained to the woman behind the front desk. "She's a university student volunteer."

The women looked down and ran a finger down a printout. "She's in ICU."

"Thanks," Nancy said quickly, dashing for the elevator to the second floor.

Once she reached the big ICU waiting room,

she picked up the red phone and asked for Ginny.

"Hi, Nancy," Ginny said, when she finally got on the line. "Sorry it took me so long to pick up. We got a bunch of critical patients in all at once, and we've been frantic."

"Did you find out anything about the tablet?" Nancy asked urgently.

"No," Ginny replied. "The lab's really backed up, too. I'm afraid it's going to be a while. I'm sorry about that."

"That's okay," Nancy told her friend, trying not to sound too dejected.

"We did get Rick's health records back from the university clinic though," Ginny added.

"Did the doctors learn anything from them?"

"Not really," Ginny replied. "Rick checked in with flulike symptoms about three weeks ago. They took some blood and cultured his throat, but they didn't find anything exotic. Just a virus. And he didn't come back for any follow-up appointments."

"Thanks, Ginny," Nancy said. She hung up the phone and let out a frustrated sigh. There wasn't anything more she could do now and she hated having her hands tied until she had more information about the tablet. That could take days.

Reluctantly, she got on the elevator.

As Nancy made her way to the exit on the ground floor, she noticed a young couple huddled together in a small space on a long bench in the waiting room. The guy and girl looked young—

several years younger than Nancy—and they were engrossed in each other.

Unexpectedly, Nancy felt a pang. Something about their closeness made her think of herself and Ned a couple years before.

Stop it! Nancy scolded herself sharply. Stop thinking about him.

But when Nancy climbed into her car and shut the door a few minutes later, she was still thinking about Ned Nickerson.

Why had it hurt her so deeply to see Bess embracing Ned? Was it because she was still in love with him? Was that why she'd broken up with Jake Collins, too? Because she hadn't been over Ned?

There was only one way to find out.

Nancy started the engine of her car and checked her watch. She'd make a quick phone call to see if Ned was there. If she drove nonstop, she could be on the Emerson College campus in a few hours.

"Nancy?" she heard Ned's voice behind the door.

Nancy knocked again. "Yeah, it's me."

The door opened, and Ned was standing there in sweats, holding a book. Nancy couldn't help smiling. His dark hair was rumpled and he looked tired and out of sorts. But his eyes were warm and familiar. "You made good time," Ned said softly. He held open the door. "Come on in."

Nancy shook her head, suddenly feeling shy. "Let's walk. I could use some fresh air."

"Sure," Ned said, and for a moment their eyes locked. "Let me pull on a sweater."

"I'm sorry to burst in on you like this," Nancy said a few moments later as they were walking down the front steps of his frat house. "I just needed to see you."

"I know," Ned said quietly. He slowed and took her by the arm. "I needed to see you, too. I think we need to talk."

Nancy took a deep breath. The air was cold and a pale moon hung over the Emerson campus. She stopped and looked at him. "I've been doing a lot of thinking, Ned."

"Me, too," Ned said gently.

"When we broke up," Nancy went on, "I think we were both a little angry. Maybe scared. I don't think we really knew what we were doing."

"Yeah." Ned sighed. "I was pretty awful. I took it as a personal affront every time you had something to do besides talk to me on the phone. I couldn't get used to the idea that there were things in your new life that I didn't know about."

Nancy smiled as they started walking toward a fountain in the middle of the campus quad. "And I think I enjoyed my new independence. We were playing games with each other."

Ned smiled back before his face turned serious again. "It hasn't been easy without you, Nan," he said softly.

Nancy sucked in her breath sharply. "It hasn't

been easy for me either," she blurted out. "When I saw you with Bess the other night, I . . ." Suddenly the words tumbled out as she explained how upset and hurt she'd felt.

"I'd go back with you in a minute, Nan," Ned said.

Nancy nodded. "That's why I'm here. I need to figure out how I feel and what to do about our relationship. It's tearing me apart."

Ned sat down next to her along the ledge of the fountain. "I've been watching your face, and you look different somehow."

"I do?" Nancy asked. Ned had always been able to read her—sometimes better than she could read herself.

"Yeah. Grown-up or something." He took her chin in his hand. "Look at me and tell me—is it over between us?"

Slowly Nancy gazed at him. And what she saw was a face that she loved with all her heart. A lump gathered in her throat as she reached up to touch his cheek. Ned. He was so familiar and such a good friend.

Suddenly what she wanted, or needed, to do was clear.

"I love you, Ned," she started. Something flickered in his eyes as she went on. "But . . ." Nancy struggled to finish. "We were together for so long. I think I have to let go for a while and let myself try out new things."

Ned let out a long disappointed sigh that nearly pierced her heart. His face was so sad. "I know you're right," he said. "I know that we both need to go our separate ways for a while, and then maybe someday . . ." He stared into her eyes.

"Maybe," Nancy said tenderly.

"It's taken me all week to figure this out, but all this time it's felt more like we were in the middle of a fight, instead of being—"

"Really apart," Ned finished her sentence.

"I know. I don't think I've ever really believed it either. I know I've never accepted it," she added ruefully.

Nancy took Ned's hand. To her surprise, she felt as though an enormous weight had been lifted. Even though it was painful to let go of Ned, it was also a relief to figure out where the two of them stood.

Ned squeezed her hand. "I still hope we find each other again someday."

"Me, too," Nancy said. "We'll have to see what the future holds." For a few minutes the two of them just sat together in silence. Nancy hadn't felt that calm in weeks. She and Ned were definitely not a couple anymore. But it was okay. She was ready to be on her own.

Ned chuckled. "Even though you didn't tell me what I wanted to hear, I'm glad you dragged me away from studying for my bio test."

Nancy smiled, then found herself telling him about the story she'd been working on.

"Oh, yeah." Ned nodded. "I read about the Wilder team in the paper last week. It sounds like

Chuck Hayes has been putting fire under your runners' heels."

Nancy looked at him. "You know Coach Hayes?"

Ned shrugged. "I've heard about him. We had a meet against St. Vincent's a couple of weeks ago, and I ran into some guys in the locker room."

Nancy waited to hear the rest of what Ned was saying.

"St. Vincent's spends a lot of money on its sports programs and the athletes are used to winning. But the cross-country team's record is poor this season. They lost against Emerson, and the guys in the locker room were bummed. Apparently they had a better year under Coach Hayes."

Nancy nodded. "Coach Hayes is a really great coach and a nice guy. It's too bad St. Vincent's lost him."

Ned looked at her. "Actually, it's too bad *Hayes* lost St. Vincent's. Its coaches' salaries and athletic scholarships are legendary. According to these runners, Hayes apparently left pretty suddenly. I got the impression that St. Vincent's didn't exactly give him a gold watch and a retirement party."

Nancy froze. "What?"

"Yeah," Ned said. "I think Hayes needed to find a new job."

"You think he was forced out?" Nancy asked, stunned.

"That was definitely the feeling I got," Ned replied.

CHAPTER 11

"Stephanie?"

"Yeah?" Stephanie was in Jonathan's bathroom, drying her hair and wondering whether it was too long for a loose wave permanent. "What are you doing here? I thought you left for work."

Jonathan opened the door. "We have to talk."

Stephanie looked at him. Jonathan looked pale and upset, completely different from his normal, cheerful self. "What's wrong? Did someone die?"

Jonathan gestured toward the living room. "No."

She dragged a comb slowly through her hair, then sat down on the couch where he was pointing. "Jonathan. Don't look at me that way."

But Jonathan's expression didn't change. His lips formed a tight line as he drew out a slip of yellow paper from his pocket. "I just found this."

"So?" Stephanie nodded. "That's the charge slip for our wedding flowers. I left it out for you."

Jonathan stared at the slip. "Eight hundred ninety-three dollars and seventy-eight cents?"

"Is that what it came to?" Stephanie asked. "I didn't check the receipt."

Stephanie grimaced as Jonathan's mouth dropped open. "You're kidding me, aren't you?"

"Well, no, actually," Stephanie admitted. "I'm sorry, Jonathan. Is that too much?"

"Yes, it's too much," Jonathan stated loudly. His face was scarlet. He turned on his heel and put a hand on his forehead.

Stephanie bit her lip. "I guess you're mad."

Jonathan slowly turned to face her. "Do you realize how long it's going to take me to pay this off?" he asked in a low voice.

"It's our wedding!" Stephanie cried out. "Don't you want it to be special?"

"Yes," Jonathan said. "I do want it to be special. But we can't afford to spend this kind of money on flowers."

Stephanie's heart fell. "Oh."

"Look," Jonathan said, sitting down next to her and taking her hands. "I know your dad's very wealthy and you've been used to the very best in life. But—I don't think I'll ever be able to compete with him."

Stephanie blinked at him.

"What I mean is," Jonathan went on, "if we're going to make it together, we're going to have to make joint decisions about money. And we'll have to be careful."

"You're probably right," Stephanie mumbled.

"There's no probably, Steph. We have to be very careful with our finances."

Stephanie looked down as tears flooded her eyes. "I just wanted our wedding to be perfect."

"But, Stephanie," Jonathan said, "we don't even have a place for the ceremony yet."

"I know," Stephanie wailed, staring up at the water stains on the apartment ceiling. "Everything's falling apart."

"Come on." Jonathan edged closer. "It'll work out."

"I can always go down to the grocery store and get a few pots of mums." Stephanie sniffled. "They've got little corsages there, too. They're in the *produce* section," she sobbed.

"Come on, stop crying," Jonathan said, softening. "Look. If we can still work out a Wednesday wedding, and if you still have your heart set on it, we can keep the flower order."

"Oh, Jonathan," Stephanie cried, flinging her arms around his neck. "I'll never forget this."

"But from now on," he insisted between Stephanie's long kisses, "we're—going—to—have to stick—to a—budget."

"Is this an off-the-record rendezvous?" Judd asked, grinning. It was Monday noon. Nancy looked up as he slid into the seat across from her at the Copacetic Carrot.

"Hey, Judd!" she said, glad to see him. "I've been trying to track you down all weekend."

Judd nodded. "I got the message you left on my machine."

"We never did finish that interview," she said. For a moment their eyes locked.

He is so handsome, Nancy thought. His blond hair was combed back, and his skin looked golden against his white shirt.

"Sorry it took me so long to find you," he said softly.

Just then the waitress came with menus, and they both ordered freshly squeezed orange juice.

"I heard that Rick's off the ventilator," Nancy said. "They think he might be okay."

"He's coming around," Judd replied happily. "Coach told us this morning. He said his family had arrived, too."

"Did the coach tell you they didn't find any drugs or alcohol in Rick's blood?" Nancy asked. "It looks like it was a viral infection of the heart."

"Uh—ah," Judd said, "the coach made quite a point of telling all of us that fact."

"Look," Nancy began carefully. "I ran into some of your teammates yesterday morning."

Judd looked up sharply, his blue eyes suddenly worried. "Hey, they're not giving you a bad time about the article you're writing, are they?"

"Actually, they are." Nancy searched his face. "They're giving me a very hard time. Did they tell you?"

He set his elbow down on the table and looked off for a second. "Not really."

"They seemed worried that I would write a story implicating Rick as a drug user," Nancy said dryly. "They don't want the team to get any bad press."

"Rick's not a drug user!" Judd said angrily.

Nancy shrugged. "It's a natural assumption after a guy like him has heart failure on a dance floor."

"It was a virus!" Judd blurted out.

Nancy stared at him, trying to figure out why he seemed so agitated. "I know that, Judd. But I still don't understand why Rudy and Lance and the others are acting so defensively. They're hiding something. They seem to be worried about their scholarships. What's going on?"

Judd stirred uncomfortably. "They're upset about Rick, Nancy. You're making too much of this."

"No, I'm not," she started to say, and then she decided to change the subject. She didn't want to spend the day arguing with Judd. "Why is Coach Hayes at Wilder?" she asked him. "He had a good job at St. Vincent's, and his team was ranked near the top."

"Coach Hayes came back to this area to help with his ailing parents," Judd said. "There was a job open at Wilder. Everyone knows that. Come on, Nancy. Do your story on the team, not on the coach's personal life. Please."

Nancy let it drop, but inside she was still wondering about the coach's sudden departure from

St. Vincent's. Ned had made it sound as if Coach Hayes had been fired.

Why? she thought. Why would a university that invested a lot of money in its sports programs dump a well-liked coach with a winning record?

Judd rubbed his face. "Speaking of St. Vincent's—we have a meet with them in a couple of days." He shook his head. "Rick's going to be bummed. He really wanted to face those guys."

Nancy did a double take. "You guys are competing against St. Vincent's?"

"Yeah," Judd said. "They're very tough. Coach Hayes taught them well. But they're in a slump."

Nancy's mind was racing. The visiting St. Vincent's runners were just the guys she needed to talk to. They could tell her if Coach Hayes had been kicked out.

Judd downed his juice. "I'm planning on going over to the hospital later. I'm hoping Rick's parents will let me see him."

"Maybe they will, now that he's out of danger," Nancy said.

"I still can't believe his heart quit on him," Judd said. "He's only eighteen years old. A year younger than I am. He hadn't been feeling well for a couple of weeks, but I never thought that something as insignificant as—"

Nancy froze. "As what?" she asked quietly.

Judd quickly started gathering his things to go. "It's just hard for me to believe that someone as young and fit as Rick could have his heart give out on him," Judd went on.

"But—"

Judd suddenly glanced at his watch. "Whoops. I'd better get going, Nancy. I'm sorry, but Coach Hayes called a special team meeting. I don't want to be late."

Nancy grabbed his wrist as Judd stood to leave. "I know you're hiding something, Judd," she said softly. "And I'm sure you have your reasons. But I want to help. Believe me. That's all I'm trying to do."

"I know, Nancy," Judd answered. For a moment Nancy thought he was going to say something more. Instead he whirled around and walked away.

"Tennessee Williams!" visiting director Jeanne Glasseburg burst out, as she sailed into Bess's advanced drama class.

Bess sat up straight in her seat as Ms. Glasseburg set her books down with a flourish and faced the small informal group. Her hair looked charmingly disheveled, and she wore a long dark skirt and oversize gray sweater. A colorful scarf was fastened with a huge silver pin at her neck.

Bess adored Ms. Glasseburg. She was a prominent New York director who had held auditions earlier for an advanced acting workshop. Luckily, Bess, Brian, Casey, and a few others had been accepted into the workshop.

It was Bess's favorite class.

"I believe he was our greatest American playwright," Ms. Glasseburg went on. "Tennessee Williams was inspired to write this play, not by the great events of history or men of power, but by his real-life sister, Rose, a fragile, unstable woman whom he cared for all of his life."

Bess thought back over the lines she'd memorized for her scene.

"Bess Marvin has agreed to perform the part of Amanda in one of the most powerful scenes from *The Glass Menagerie,*" Ms. Glasseburg said. "Amanda's monologue is in the sixth scene."

Bess smoothed back her hair, then stood up and walked to the empty performing space.

"In this scene," Ms. Glasseburg filled the class in, "the narrator's mother is reminiscing about her lost youth."

Bess drew in a deep breath and tried to push away her fear. It felt good to be there, in spite of her nervousness.

"You may begin when you're ready, Bess," Ms. Glasseburg said quietly.

Bess looked out at the small group of her theater colleagues. Brian winked and gave her a thumbs-up sign.

Bess began to speak her lines. As she said the words, she could feel herself transforming into the character of Amanda. Her voice rose, growing stronger. There was nothing to be nervous about now. Bess could already tell that this performance would be one of her best.

* * *

"People!" Gail Gardeski cried, standing up on her desk chair so the entire news room could see her. She cupped her hands around her mouth. "Please use the spell-check before you submit your articles!"

Nancy winced as she hurried to her own desk. Monday afternoons were always chaotic at the *Times,* since everyone was always way behind after a weekend of partying.

"Hey, Blackburn," Gail boomed, whipping her glasses off and glaring across the room. "There's an *n* in the word *government.* Burn that into your brain—okay?"

Nancy headed straight for her computer and dumped her bookbag on the floor. The first thing she wanted to do was log on to the Internet to find a news-clipping site. If Ned was right and Coach Hayes had been fired from St. Vincent's, then she wanted to know why. If he'd been using illegal techniques or drugs to boost team performances, he could be doing the same thing at Wilder.

Nancy grabbed an apple from her bag, bit into it, and began a search for the Lakewood daily newspaper. Lakewood was where St. Vincent's was located, and the local sports section was sure to have university sports coverage.

"Bingo," Nancy said after a half hour of searching. "Here's something." She scanned the headline.

"St. Vincent's team in slump following retirement of legendary coach Chuck Hayes." The article went on to mention the runners' sagging times and low team morale, which followed directly after Hayes's departure.

Nancy sat back and looked at the ceiling. She remembered the *Times* article about the way Hayes had dramatically turned around the Wilder team after his arrival. The stunning times. The sudden wild expectation that the Norsemen would win the regionals. What was it? What did Chuck Hayes have? Magic? she wondered.

"Intercampus mail for you," a student with a mail bag said, interrupting her thoughts.

"Thanks," Nancy said, taking the manila envelope. She turned it over. The envelope was addressed to Nancy Drew, c/o *Wilder Times* news room. There was no return address.

She unwound the string attached to the envelope flap and drew out a printed note.

Dear Nancy,

Why do you think the Wilder men's cross-country team is doing so well this year?

Abruptly, Nancy stood up and looked around the room. Who could have sent this to her? None of the reporters in the sports department was around. She sat down and finished reading.

It's worth looking into. Turnarounds like this don't just happen. This team couldn't have done it without a certain friend and a coach who took advantage.

Keep digging, Nancy.

Anonymous

Nancy slowly lowered the note. She'd hardly told anyone about her investigation. And yet someone out there knew exactly what she was doing.

As she reread the typed note, a chill traveled up her spine.

"This team couldn't have done it without a certain friend and a coach who took advantage."

What in the world did that mean?

Stephanie had skipped every single one of her Monday classes.

Since her argument with Jonathan that morning, she'd stomped downtown to Selena's, an upscale dress shop, where she'd tried on at least a dozen outfits and left without buying a thing. She didn't have her dad's credit card. And she definitely didn't have Jonathan's. All she had was the money in her wallet—exactly thirty-two dollars and seventy-two cents.

It wasn't enough to buy clothes, but it was enough to buy a half-price facial and cosmetic makeover, which the shop next door was offering.

After she'd spent all her money, Stephanie wandered back to campus, where she ripped into a fresh pack of cigarettes and walked around the lake several times.

This was supposed to be the happiest time of her life. Instead she and Jonathan had just had a major fight.

We made up, she reminded herself. He even said you didn't have to cancel the flower order.

Still Stephanie worried that Jonathan was already sick of her. And she also kept thinking about her dad. He cared so little about her that he refused to attend her wedding.

What am I doing? she wondered.

Stephanie took a deep drag on her cigarette and blew out the smoke. Everyone—including her friends—thought her wedding plans were a big joke.

"They don't care about me," Stephanie said suddenly. "And neither does Jonathan."

Stephanie walked faster, oblivious to the runners and other college students all around her. "Why should I care?" she mumbled out loud. "No one else does. Maybe I'll call off the wedding, drop out of school, and move to a big city, where I can get a job."

There'd be no attachments, she thought, lifting her head defiantly. No risks. No commitments. No pain.

Feeling a lot more settled, Stephanie hurried back to Thayer Hall, where she would phone Jonathan and call off the wedding. She would then spend the night at Club Z picking up the cutest guy she could find.

The dorm elevator dinged as it stopped on the third floor, then opened into a pitch-black hall. "What—" Impatiently, Stephanie groped for the switch to turn the lights on in the lounge to Suite 301.

"Surprise!" Voices rang out.

Stephanie drew her hands up to her face in shock. The lounge, usually deserted just before dinner, was filled with people. Bunting and paper flowers had been tacked to the walls and there was a long handmade banner that read "Congratulations, Stephanie and Jonathan!"

"Oh my . . ." Stephanie gasped.

Platters of cold cuts, fruit, and breads were laid out on a side table, surrounding a beautiful white cake.

"Come on, Steph, say something!" Casey yelled, giving her a big hug.

But Stephanie couldn't speak. Tears sprouted in her eyes as she took in the presents heaped on the coffee table, and the people in the room—Liz, Ginny, Nancy, Kara, Casey, Dawn, Reva, Eileen.

"I—I don't know what to say. . . ." Stephanie stammered. She was so surprised, she didn't know what to think.

"It's the first time that Stephanie Keats has ever been at a loss for words," Liz joked.

Stephanie wiped her eyes. "I just can't believe it," she said. "Thanks so much—and let's dig in, okay?"

"All right!" Dawn called out. "But you have to open your presents first."

Stephanie settled on the couch and Nancy handed her a box wrapped in silver paper.

With trembling fingers, Stephanie opened it to find a filmy white nightgown. It was from Nancy, Dawn, Kara, and Eileen. There was also a bubble bath set from Liz, a pair of satin slippers from Reva, and three beautiful pairs of stockings from Ginny.

Finally there was Casey's present: a large, white box surrounded by silver ribbon. Stephanie opened it and drew out a long silky robe that exactly matched the nightgown.

"Thank you, Casey," she whispered. "It's beautiful." Then she turned to face the whole group. "Thank you, everyone," she said softly. "I'm sorry I've been so testy lately."

"Mmmmm," Kara said, rolling her eyes. "You?"

A few people giggled.

"All you have to do is invite us to the wedding, day after tomorrow," Nancy piped up.

Stephanie felt her smile fade. "To tell you the truth, I don't know if we're going to pull this off in time. We still don't have a place to get married."

"Oh, yes, you do," Casey told her.

Stephanie looked at her in surprise.

Casey's eyes were sparkling back. "The Kappas have invited you and Jonathan to have your wedding at their house on Wednesday night."

Stephanie felt her heart jump into her throat with joy. "What?"

Casey repeated the news. "So you're *really* going to have to get ready now, pal," she said. "You're getting married in forty-eight hours."

Stephanie was so shocked and touched by her friends' generosity that she covered her eyes with her hands. The day had started out badly, but in the last few minutes, things had changed—dramatically. This had actually turned out to be one of the happiest days of her life.

CHAPTER 12

I'm looking for Coach Hayes's office," Nancy told the student behind the front desk at the university athletic center the next day.

"Basement, Room Ten-thirty-three, next to the laundry room," the guy said, looking up from a clipboard.

"Thanks," Nancy replied.

"But if they win the regional championships," the guy added with a twinkle in his eye, "you'll want to look for his office on the third floor, next to the director's."

Nancy smiled back, then headed for the stairway.

After receiving the anonymous note and reading about the coach's record at St. Vincent's, Nancy was looking forward to talking with Coach Hayes. She had a hard time believing that someone as well-liked as Hayes could have been kicked out of a university—or have something to do with pills in a gym bag.

Nancy found Room 1033 right away. The name *Chuck Hayes* was painted on the blue door.

"Is there something I can help you with, miss?" a voice said as she entered.

Coach Hayes sat behind his desk. As he looked up, Nancy noticed he'd been collecting some items from a drawer and putting them in a gym bag.

"I'm Nancy Drew with the *Wilder Times,* the campus paper," she started.

Coach Hayes slapped a hand on his forehead. "Nancy. Of course. I'm so sorry I didn't recognize you right away." He came around the desk to shake her hand warmly. "I was pretty upset about Rick when we met in that hospital waiting room. Please sit down."

Nancy smiled politely. "I'm doing an article for the newspaper about your team, Coach Hayes," she explained.

He nodded. "They are a sensational bunch of athletes."

"I'll say," Nancy agreed. "They've won every meet this year and seem to be headed for the regionals. The focus of my story is their success— and how you've turned them around."

"That sounds great," the coach said. "But I hope you'll focus on the kids—they've been working their hearts out and deserve the real attention."

"Do you have time for an interview right now?" Nancy asked.

Coach Hayes looked at his watch and made

a face. "Unfortunately, I have a meeting at the director's office that was supposed to start five minutes ago."

Nancy nodded. "How about tomorrow afternoon at this time?"

"Sure," Coach Hayes replied. "Why don't you walk with me to the elevator? Maybe I can answer a few of your questions on the way."

"Great," Nancy replied. She turned toward the hallway while Coach Hayes grabbed a canvas briefcase and turned off his desk lamp.

Nancy was about to start for the door when the small notebook she was holding slipped from her fingers. As she bent down to pick it up, she spotted a brown paper bag on the floor filled with several small plastic bottles. Her eyes caught some of the lettering on one of the bottles: D-E-R-O-N.

Slowly Nancy stood up. Her legs felt wooden as she followed the coach out the door into the hallway.

"I'm the luckiest man in the world," he was saying.

Nancy barely heard him. Her thoughts were racing. Was there a connection between the bottles she'd just seen and the pill she'd found in Rudy's gym bag? Or was her imagination running away with her?

"You see," the coach continued, "I love this sport. I was a long-distance runner myself in college. At St. Vincent's we had several gifted freshmen who stayed with it all four years and took well to my style of training."

"Oh." Nancy managed to turn her attention back to the coach. "What style is that?"

Coach Hayes punched the elevator button. "I work on keeping the runners' attitudes positive. I work on basic technique. I try to get to know my runners and figure out what makes them tick. They're not machines. They're kids with baggage. Kids with grades to keep up. Kids who want to have fun."

"Do you drive them hard?" Nancy asked.

"Oh, yeah," he said. "That's how you produce winners. I drive them *very* hard." The elevator opened and Coach Hayes waved goodbye. "We'll talk some more tomorrow."

Nancy waved back. "You drive them pretty hard—mmm?" she muttered after the elevator doors had closed again. "How hard is that? Too hard for Rick Alexander?"

Bess slowly opened the front door of the Hewlitt Performing Arts Center. The long first-floor hall was empty except for a few scattered dancers in leotards and a guy checking the audition board near the main rehearsal hall.

Ms. Glasseburg had called her an hour ago and asked her to stop by her office at four o'clock. Bess couldn't figure out what the drama teacher wanted.

Maybe she hated my monologue from *The Glass Menagerie*, Bess worried. I thought I did it well, but maybe she thought it was so bad that she's going to kick me out of the program.

"Bess!" Ms. Glasseburg was smiling as Bess opened the door to her office. She was on the phone and motioned for Bess to sit down.

"Tell Tony I want those set designs faxed to me by tomorrow then," Ms. Glasseburg barked into the phone. "We've got rehearsals in six weeks and a construction crew sitting on its hands waiting to get going!"

Bess sat anxiously until the teacher hung up the phone.

"Now," Ms. Glasseburg said. "I liked your Amanda monologue very much."

Whew, Bess thought, trying to hide her relief. "Thank you," she said calmly.

"I wanted to tell you that because I've been worried about you for the past couple weeks," Ms. Glasseburg went on.

"You have?" Bess bit her lip.

"You've seemed very distracted lately," she continued. "But yesterday you were completely focused. You did that scene beautifully, and it's not an easy scene to do. Many people think it is, but it's not. Believe me, I know. I've performed the part many times myself. Your interpretation was sensitive, moving and played with a maturity far beyond your years."

Bess beamed as Ms. Glasseburg continued praising her.

"So," the teacher went on briskly. "I'm filling you up with all of these ego-inflating compliments because I want you to do something for me."

"Sure," Bess said. She waited to hear the request.

"As you may know, I'm about to hold auditions for *Cat on a Hot Tin Roof.*"

Bess nodded. How could she not know? The show was going to be the biggest project this semester at Wilder. And, because Ms. Glasseburg was a famous Tennessee Williams authority, it was sure to be reviewed by even the Chicago critics. Everyone was talking about it.

"I'm going to start auditions beginning next week," Ms. Glasseburg said. "And I want you to audition."

"Me?" Bess couldn't believe it. "For which part?"

"For Maggie," Ms. Glasseburg said. "I'd like to see what you can do with the role."

"Oh my gosh," Bess managed to say. "Thank you." She felt as if she were dreaming as she stood up and left the office, then floated out into the hall.

Bess was thrilled. Ms. Glasseburg—a well-known New York stage actress and director—actually wanted her to audition for the lead.

"Over here," Nancy whispered to George, motioning toward the university library's computer periodical catalog.

It was early evening. After talking with Coach Hayes, Nancy had tracked down George for an early dinner, then dragged her down to the library to help her with some research.

"What are you going to look for first?" George asked.

Nancy sat down in front of one of the empty terminals, and George drew up a chair next to her. "Subject," Nancy murmured. "How about sports medicine?"

"Medicine?" George echoed.

"Just a hunch," Nancy said as she typed and entered her file request. "I can't get those bottles in Coach Hayes's office out of my head."

George shrugged. "It could have been anything, Nancy. Athletes are always taking vitamin and mineral supplements. And lots of runners are into herbal remedies for everything from muscle pain to stress and depression."

Nancy scanned the entries that appeared on the screen.

"What were those letters you saw on the bottle?" George asked.

"D-E-R-O-N," Nancy answered.

George made a face. "That doesn't sound very organic."

"Nope. It sounds more like—"

"Something you'd put in your car's engine," George jumped in.

Nancy laughed, then started to read some of the titles aloud. " 'Injury Prevention' . . . 'Joint Replacement.' "

"Neither of those," George said, shaking her head.

" 'Therapeutic Sports Medicine,' 'First Aid,' 'Performance Enhancements . . .' "

"Hey, try that," George suggested, pointing to "Performance Enhancements." "Your story is about the team's incredible winning streak, isn't it?"

"Yes," Nancy said. Eagerly, she entered the request. A second later she read the lists of available magazine and newspaper articles on enhancing performance. "These are stories about nutritional supplements, steroids, amphetamines, strengthening . . . Oh."

"What?"

Nancy clicked on the last category. "Check this out," she said. "It's a *Sports Monthly* article from last year. 'University study links caffeine intake to speed on the athletic fields.' The story's in the system. I'm going to print it."

"Caffeine?" George scoffed. "Come on."

Nancy shrugged as she waited for the article to drop into the printer tray.

Then she scooped up the first page and started reading.

" 'University researchers have discovered that caffeine in high doses can boost speed and concentration among athletes in nearly all sports.' "

George wrinkled her nose. "You'd have to drink a lot of coffee or cola to get a really high dose," she commented. "Or"—she looked at Nancy—"take a lot of those little caffeine pills you can buy to help you stay awake when you have to study."

Nancy stared at George for a second. They were both wondering the same thing. " 'In controlled experiments,' " Nancy went on reading, " 'volunteer athletes given doses in excess of two hundred fifty milligrams were able to increase running speeds, for example, by up to twenty-five percent.' "

Up to twenty-five percent?

Nancy stared at the article in amazement. Could the team possibly be taking high doses of caffeine before the meets? It would certainly explain the tablet in the gym bag and the bottles in the coach's office.

But what about Rick's heart failure? Nancy wondered. Could something as seemingly harmless as caffeine actually cause someone's heart to stop?

"Come on," George said abruptly. "Let's get out of here. This whole thing makes me sick."

Nancy nodded, then shoved the article in her backpack. She had a feeling that she was finally getting closer to understanding what was going on at the track.

When George and Nancy entered Nancy's dorm a short time later, they found Kara in one of her yoga stretching positions in the middle of the room.

"Hi," Kara said. "Got your story under control, Nancy?"

"Maybe," Nancy said. She told Kara about what they'd found.

"Maybe this will help," Kara said. She leaned

over to pick up a manila intercampus mail envelope from her bed.

"It's from Anonymous again," Nancy mumbled, quickly unwinding the string closure.

Dear Nancy,
I know that your investigation hasn't been easy. But it's very important that you stay with it. Don't give up—for Rick's sake.

George read the unsigned note over her shoulder.

"This note tells me absolutely nothing," Nancy said, disappointed. "I wish I could at least figure out who's sending the notes."

"Hey," George said as she glanced again at the sheet of paper. "Did you notice something distinctive about this person's printer?"

"What do you . . ." Nancy's words trailed off as she saw what George meant. Like the first note, this one had been printed on a laser printer, and the bottom of the page had a dark line running across it. She remembered that her father's printer back home had once left the same mark when it needed a new ink cartridge.

"Good observation," Nancy told George. "If I could track down that printer, I'd find my friend Anonymous."

Just then the phone rang and Nancy grabbed it.

"Nancy? It's Ginny. I'm at the hospital."

"Are the lab tests back on the tablet?" Nancy asked eagerly.

"Yes," Ginny said excitedly. "Alison came through and did a quick analysis for me. Plus, I've got one of our cardiologists here and she wants to talk to you about it. Her name's Dr. Sheila Horowitz. Get down to the cardiac unit as fast as you can."

"When Ginny told me what you were working on, I wanted to help," Dr. Horowitz said.

"Thank you," Nancy said, catching her breath. "I practically flew down here."

Dr. Horowitz picked up the lab report and examined it. She was a woman in her forties with curly brown hair and wire-rimmed glasses. "The pill you found was pure caffeine," she confirmed.

Nancy wasn't surprised. But she still wasn't sure what to do with this information. "Caffeine seems so innocent," she told the doctor. "Can it really affect people's performances?"

"Absolutely," Dr. Horowitz replied. "The tablet you brought in for analysis contained five hundred milligrams of caffeine."

"Is that a lot?" Nancy asked.

"Imagine a strong cup of coffee," Dr. Horowitz said, her direct blue eyes fixed on Nancy's. "That's about sixty milligrams."

"So that one pill is equal to more than eight cups," Ginny reasoned.

"Yes," the doctor went on. "Some athletes have been known to take one of these pills before a competition to improve their performance.

Some might take one. But others may take two or three."

"What does it do?" Nancy asked, taking out her notebook.

"It increases the heart rate," Dr. Horowitz explained. "But if the heart is weak or has been weakened by a viral infection, then the caffeine could aggravate the weakened heart, causing an atrial fibrillation—or worse: heart failure," Dr. Horowitz explained. "Which is exactly what happened to your friend."

"Oh, my gosh," Nancy murmured.

"It's a real problem with our young athletes," Dr. Horowitz went on. "Because some of them will do anything to win. And they think caffeine is harmless. You can buy it at some drugstores under the brand name Dexederon, but it's definitely not safe in high dosages, especially if the body's defenses are down."

D-E-R-O-N. Nancy felt sick as she recognized the letters from the bottle under Coach Hayes's desk. It all made sense now. Obviously, the coach wanted to win so badly, he was supplying the team with the pills to improve their performances. Is that the reason he departed so abruptly from St. Vincent's, too? she wondered.

"People need to know about this hazard—especially our young athletes," the doctor said. "Your friend on the cross-country team could have died. In fact, there's a very good chance his athletic career is over. With extensive heart damage, he could even die within a few years, unless he gets a heart transplant."

Ginny put her hand on Nancy's shoulder. "That's why Dr. Horowitz got really interested when I told her about this. This isn't the first time she's seen caffeine overdoses."

"You'd be doing everyone a real service by reporting this danger," Dr. Horowitz stressed.

Nancy pressed her lips together.

Now that she had her story, she almost didn't want it. But she knew Dr. Horowitz was right. She had to report the results from the lab test—before another life was endangered.

CHAPTER 13

"Come on in, Nancy," Coach Hayes said. He was on the phone, but he waved her good-naturedly toward a seat.

Nancy smiled and told herself to stay calm. She had her suspicions, but she hadn't proved that Coach Hayes had anything to do with the caffeine tablet that she found in the gym bag. And Ginny had pointed out that the coach could have confiscated the bottles of pills from a member of his team.

"Thanks for waiting," Coach Hayes said as he finally hung up. His desk, which had been cluttered the day before, now looked perfectly clear. As Nancy glanced behind him, she saw the walls were covered with carefully framed certificates and trophies. "Now, what more can I tell you about Wilder's incredible team?"

"How on earth did Wilder University snag you?" Nancy started.

Coach Hayes smiled broadly and sat back in his chair. "It's true that St. Vincent's was good to me, but I was ready to move on. And I wanted to be in Weston."

"From all reports, Coach, it was *you* who turned St. Vincent's team around," Nancy said, flattering him. "Just the way you're turning our team around this season."

Coach Hayes waved away the compliment. "It was good luck on both sides, Nancy. I had some fine athletes to work with at both universities. Those kids were the ones who worked hard and improved their times. I was merely the one who told them they could do it."

"Was it tough leaving St. Vincent's?" Nancy asked, watching his face closely.

Coach Hayes cleared his throat. "Yes, it was. But as I was saying, it was time to give someone else a go at St. Vincent's. And I wanted to spend time in Weston with my mom and pop."

Nancy shifted her tone a little. "Isn't it true that you've been able to get unbelievable performances out of your runners this year? I mean, their times have dropped dramatically. A lot of people have even called it a miracle."

Coach Hayes's eyes narrowed.

"How did you do it?" Nancy went on.

"It's a combination of things: conditioning, precision weight training, technique—and attitude," the coach came back.

Nancy wrote down everything he said. "Do

you recommend vitamin or herbal supplements to boost energy levels?"

"That's the individual runner's own choice," he said, slowing picking up a pen and tapping it on the surface of his desk.

Nancy gave him a level stare. "I have information that at least one of your players carries a supply of a high-dose caffeine product called Dexederon."

Coach Hayes completely dropped his friendly exterior. "What do you think you're doing?" he growled.

Nancy lifted her chin. "A cardiologist at Weston General has examined Rick Alexander's records—"

"Are you trying to tell me that you think I had something to do with what happened to Rick?" Coach Hayes demanded.

"I don't know what to think," Nancy said simply. "But the doctor said his heart failure could easily have been induced by a high-dose caffeine tablet like the one that I discovered last weekend. I had it analyzed, you see."

Coach Hayes slowly stood up and raised his arm. He pointed toward the door, shaking with fury. "You—get—out—of—here," he said in a low threatening voice. "I have nothing to say to you. And my team members don't either. I intend to remind them that you are trying to tarnish the reputation of this team, not to mention my reputation and Rick Alexander's."

"Rick nearly lost his life on Friday," Nancy shot back. "And people want to know why."

Coach Hayes just stood there, his hands trembling and his lip curled in anger. "If you pursue this sicko idea of yours any further, young lady, you'd better watch your back."

He just incriminated himself! Nancy thought racing out of the athletic center across campus toward Jasper Hall, where Judd lived. She had to talk to him right away.

"I know the coach did it," Nancy whispered grimly. "I wouldn't put it past him to feed his runners drugs to boost his own reputation."

She knew from reading about the team that runners like Rudy Milton and Lance Macon had been only mediocre last year. Athletes with lackluster performances can easily lose their scholarships, Nancy reflected, especially if their grades are weak, too. The drive to win and hold on to their scholarships could have easily made some runners turn to shortcuts. Maybe that was exactly what Rudy, Lance, and the others had done.

Maybe what Judd had done, too, Nancy acknowledged. She found herself trying not to think of his involvement in the affair.

Nancy drew her jacket collar up around her neck as a gust of cold wind whipped up. Dusk was falling as she headed toward the quad.

What was she going to say to him when she saw him? Should she just blurt out all the evidence she'd discovered?

Nancy glanced around, wishing she knew where Jasper Hall was. She finally noticed a sign pointing to the right, but as she got closer, she realized she'd gone the back way. The path was worn away and poorly lit.

Nancy stopped for a second look around. Jasper Hall was a slightly run-down men's dorm, surrounded by huge trees and garbage cans lined up behind the building. Nancy was startled by a stray cat suddenly dashing out in front of her.

"Whoa! You scared me," she cried, her heart thumping in her chest. Just then a sound came from behind. Her veins went ice cold as a hand grabbed her shoulder—hard.

"Hey," Nancy said sharply.

The arm slammed her up against the side of the brick building. Even in the dim light, she recognized Rudy Milton, Judd's team captain. He stood glowering at her, his dark eyes angry and menacing.

"Let me go!" Nancy ordered him.

But Rudy kept her pinned with his powerful arm. "Not before I give you a message," he said in a threatening tone. "I happened to stop by Coach Hayes's office a few seconds after you left, and he told me about the nasty things you said."

"I know what's going on," Nancy said, trying to shake him off. She remembered the initials on the gym bag. RM. Rudy Milton.

Rudy sneered. "Everyone knows you've been seeing Judd Wright. Now—if you spread false rumors about the team, I'll tell you what I'm going to do."

Nancy glared at him. "What's that?"

"I'll tell the administration that Judd is deliberately spreading false rumors to the press, and Judd will get dropped from the team. And of course he'll lose that scholarship he depends on," Rudy went on.

Nancy yanked her arm away. "You'd never get away with that, Rudy. Coach Hayes is the one who's going to get dropped."

"You're wrong, Nancy. The people here at Wilder really like Coach Hayes and all the alumni support bringing him in. They're not about to blow the chance to bring in big bucks for the university."

"They will when they find out what he's been doing," Nancy shot back.

"If you print these lies you'll spoil everything we've worked for," Rudy hissed in her ear. "Now, get off our backs—we've got an important meet tomorrow, and we want you out of our faces." He glared at her as he let go of her arm and started to back away.

"I'll be watching you" was his final warning before he disappeared into the darkness.

"Judd!" Nancy shouted. She was banging on his room door with her fist. After running up three flights of stairs, she was panting and beads of sweat had broken out on her forehead. "Judd! Are you there?"

The door suddenly swung open. "Nancy! What's wrong?" Judd gasped.

Nancy drew her hands up to her face and realized that she was shaking all over.

"Nancy?" Judd said gently, pulling her into the room. "Come in and sit down."

She dropped down on the edge of Judd's bed. She couldn't believe Rudy Milton had just threatened her.

"It's okay," Judd said, sitting next to her. "Take your time."

Nancy nodded, taking several deep breaths to calm herself. Glancing around the room, she saw a neat desk in one corner. Nearby, a creaky-sounding printer was slowly spitting out pages of a document into a paper tray.

"I've just been to see Coach Hayes and . . ." Nancy began, trying to steady her voice.

"Yes?" Judd said nervously.

"I know how the coach told everyone on the team not to talk to me. He just told me. In fact he threatened me." Nancy rubbed her arm where she'd been grabbed. "And then Rudy followed me here. And he managed to get in a few more threats."

Judd faced her, his blue eyes widening with shock. "What? Did Rudy hurt you?"

"Not seriously." Nancy flexed her arm. "But he was pretty rough. He's afraid of what I know about Rick Alexander's heart failure," she went on. "And he's afraid of . . ." She looked at Judd. "What else I know."

"Oh man," Judd said softly.

"What's going on, Judd?" Nancy said. "Why did you keep all this stuff to yourself when you knew—"

"Nancy, you don't understand."

"Was it because Coach Hayes told you not to talk to me?" Nancy demanded. "How could you stay quiet—especially when your friend nearly died?"

Judd stuffed his hands in his pockets and stood up. "I'm sorry."

"You've known all along about the caffeine pills, right?" Nancy said. "That's why you were so angry with the team at Club Z."

"Nancy," Judd pleaded. "I'm on scholarship here. If I get on the wrong side of this coach, he can cut me off, just like that. I'd lose my scholarship and have to drop out. Don't you see? My parents don't have money for college."

Nancy couldn't believe what she was hearing. Doesn't anyone care about Rick Alexander? she thought. She glared at Judd. "Did you take the caffeine, too?" she asked.

He shook his head. "No. I'm not into using drugs to enhance my performance." A long silence fell between them.

Finally Nancy stood up to leave. She couldn't help feeling disappointed in Judd. Having a scholarship didn't excuse him. He still could have warned her—or at least hinted—that something was going on.

"I'm sorry," Judd repeated. There was a miserable expression on his face. "Believe it or not, I was planning to call you later to talk as soon as I finished my term paper." He nodded toward the printer, still spewing out the pages one by one.

"Yeah, well—" Nancy started. Her voice trailed off as she glanced at the printer's paper tray. Then she felt herself stop breathing. She stepped over to the printer to get a better look.

"What?" Judd said, confused. "Are you interested in the economic factors leading to the 1929 stock market crash?"

"No." As Nancy stared at the printed pages, her heart lifted. Then she looked up at Judd. "I'm interested in the high cost of getting laser printer cartridges replaced."

Judd scratched his head. "Huh?"

She pointed to the black line at the bottom of each page. "You sent me those anonymous notes," she said. "I recognize the fault in this printer. You weren't trying to hide the information—you *wanted* me to find out what was going on."

Judd stared at her, unable to speak.

Tenderness for him washed over her as she saw his eyes fill with tears. She moved toward him and he grabbed her, holding her tight. As he rocked her back and forth, she could feel his chest heaving with sobs. "Rick almost died."

"He's better now, Judd," Nancy whispered.

"Nancy," Judd said softly. "Those notes—I didn't know what else to do. I had to tell someone."

"What happened, Judd?" Nancy asked. "How did it all start?"

"Coach Hayes brought these tablets to practice one day at the beginning of the season. He said they were harmless energy boosters. Good for improving our times."

"What a creep!" Nancy declared.

"I'll say," Judd agreed. "Sure enough, some of the runners' times started to improve. Rudy was really into it—his times improved more than anyone's. But then Coach Hayes casually mentioned one day that caffeine pills were actually banned for college competitors, and discovery could cause automatic disqualification from the meets."

"Why did you keep quiet?" Nancy asked.

"He made us swear to secrecy or he'd kick us off the team. There wasn't much I could do. Plus, everyone was so happy. Times were down, and we were winning. No one told us there was a health risk."

"What happened with Rick?" Nancy asked quietly.

Judd shook his head. "About three weeks ago, as I told you, Rick got the flu. He was really flat-out for a few days, but he rallied and really wanted to get ready for a meet we had with Whitman University.

Nancy nodded. "Is that when he tried the caffeine pills?"

"Yeah." Judd sighed. "I told him to rest and lay off the stuff. But his times improved even though he'd been sick. He was convinced the stuff could pull him through his health slump. He didn't want to miss his big chance."

"He probably didn't give his body a chance to heal," Nancy said. "He had a virus in his heart that wasn't going away, but I bet the caffeine masked the symptoms. It probably kept him from going back to the clinic for treatment."

"Yeah, and then he got used to taking the stuff," Judd explained. "Rudy was into it. In fact, Rudy was practically making Rick take the stuff, his times were so amazing."

"What happened the night of the Club Z party?" Nancy asked. "When he collapsed."

"Rudy was pretty high that night because he'd taken something like three or four of these pills before the last meet, and his times were better than ever. Plus, he told everyone what an incredible rush it had given him."

Nancy put a hand on her forehead as she thought back to that terrible night.

"Everyone was popping the pills like crazy," Judd went on. "Remember the music? It was wild. Everyone was dancing and Rick must have really overdone it, too."

Nancy's mind was churning. "The same thing must have happened at St. Vincent's when Coach Hayes was there. That's probably why his team performed so well for so long. I wonder if he got caught."

Judd's blue eyes searched hers. He took her hand. "There's someone I want you to talk to."

Nancy watched as Judd dug for a slip of paper and reached for his phone.

"Brad?" Judd said softly after punching in a number. "Hi. It's Judd. Can we meet? I've got that reporter with me." A second later he hung up.

"Come on," Judd said, taking Nancy's hand. "We're meeting a friend of mine down at the Cave."

"Who?" Nancy asked as Judd dragged her out the door.

"The perfect interview, that's who," Judd said. For the first time that night, Nancy saw him smile a little.

She gave his hand a warm squeeze.

A few minutes later Nancy and Judd were hurrying into the dimly lit Cave, where about a dozen students were taking a study break to listen to music and grab coffee or a pizza.

As they entered, Judd felt a thrill that Nancy was still holding his hand. She has such incredible blue eyes and she's so smart, he thought. Suddenly he realized that he'd been thinking about her almost nonstop since the first day they'd met. Now he felt even more drawn to her.

Nancy had saved him tonight. The last few months of hiding and guilt had nearly consumed him. It had been horrible to make up excuses for the team's sudden success. Worse had been watching Rick destroy himself with the caffeine pills.

"Hey, Judd!" his old friend called out.

Judd spotted him at a small table in the corner and smiled. He really looked like a runner today, with his tall lean frame, taut face, and warm-up suit. Gently, he steered Nancy toward him.

"Hey, Brad," Judd said, turning to Nancy. "Nancy, this is my old friend Brad Hoffman. We were best of friends and the most vicious competitors in high school."

"Hello," Nancy said, looking confused.

"Back in high school, when we were all waiting to find out about colleges," Judd continued, "I thought I was really hot when Wilder offered me a full four-year scholarship. But then my friend Brad here got the St. Vincent's scholarship."

Judd watched as Nancy's eyes lit up. "You're at St. Vincent's?" She put her hand on Judd's shoulder. "Now I know why you called him the perfect interview."

"Brad's here for the meet tomorrow," Judd explained. "We got together last night and I told him about your investigation. I guess we've both hoped for a long time that this would come out."

"So talk, Brad," Nancy said soberly.

"Tell her what you know," Judd said, nodding. "Our friend Coach Hayes has it coming to him." He knew his scholarship would end if Coach Hayes won this fight. But he was pretty certain that Nancy's evidence was irrefutable. Once the school heard about the coach's connection to Rick's heart failure, Coach Hayes was not going to be the school's golden boy anymore. Instead he would be an enormous embarrassment.

"For now," Brad began, "we're off the record. There are still Chuck Hayes loyalists crawling all over the athletic department at St. Vincent's. But once the story breaks, everything can be verified with the dean's office over at St. Vincent's."

Nancy propped her elbows on the table. "So why did he leave and take on a struggling third-rate team like Wilder's?"

Brad drew a breath. "Because he was thrown out, of course. Forced to retire."

"I knew it," Nancy said.

"It got around that he was feeding his athletes caffeine tablets before meets, just as he is now, here," Brad explained.

Nancy shook her head in disgust.

"A couple of the younger guys—freshmen—had some pretty scary reactions to the stuff. The athletic director found out about it."

"Why was it such a secret?" Nancy wanted to know. "He's just brought a terribly dangerous practice over to a whole new set of runners at Wilder. Didn't St. Vincent's care?"

Brad's face grew hard. "I know. That's why I'm talking to you, Nancy. The deal Hayes got was a hush-hush retirement. Remember, his incredible record brought St. Vincent's big alumni bucks and lots of great publicity."

"The school didn't want any bad press either," Judd said.

"But now you're in the perfect position to stop

him," Brad said, pulling out a St. Vincent's University administration phone directory. "I've highlighted some names for you."

Nancy took the book. "Thanks, Brad."

Judd watched her turn to him with a serious expression. "And you know what you have to do."

Judd nodded. "I'm going to the head of the athletic department. And tell him everything that's happened."

CHAPTER 14

Stuffed mushrooms," Casey recited. "Ham-wrapped asparagus. Miniature quiches. Melon platter. And herbed bread."

Stephanie shivered with delight. She was sitting in the Kappas' large powder room on the first floor, adjusting her veil and the rosebud-covered comb that held it in place. Surrounding her were Casey's sorority sisters, Eileen, Bess, and several other Kappa assistants.

"It's going to be a beautiful wedding," Stephanie said softly as Bess fluffed out the veil. "I just can't believe it's happening."

"Believe it." Eileen giggled. "Did you hear that Soozie's mom got so excited about an on-campus wedding, she Fed-Exed her family's heirloom linen tablecloth?"

Casey grinned, examining her clipboard one last time. "Once I told the Kappas we were having a wedding, they went berserk.

I think they're fantasizing about their own weddings."

"Thanks so much for all the flowers," Stephanie said softly. "I canceled everything I'd ordered from the florist except the bouquet, and I had him make it smaller."

"I'm glad." Casey patted her. "It doesn't take a fortune to create a beautiful ceremony."

"Yeah," Stephanie said quietly. "Weddings are about love, not money, aren't they?" She was too shy to tell Casey that they were about friendship, too—something she'd just learned.

"Okay, stand up, Stephanie," Casey ordered, handing her the bouquet.

Stephanie stood before the room's full-length mirror and drew in a sharp breath. She had to admit that the white dress, which hadn't been her first choice, looked wonderful on her. It had a deep V neckline and was made of satin covered by a layer of delicate lace.

"You look beautiful," Bess breathed.

Stephanie wiped away a tear. "I don't deserve this."

"Yes, you do," Casey insisted. "You can be a ditz sometimes, Steph. But we love you anyway."

"Are you ready?" Bess asked.

"Yes," Stephanie whispered. "But I . . ."

"What, Steph?" Casey asked.

Stephanie shook her head softly, unable to speak. She knew that the heavy feeling had something to do with her father. She'd felt it all day. Her wedding day—without her father. He wouldn't walk her down the aisle. He wouldn't give her away. He didn't even know Jonathan. She wanted to tell her friends, but she couldn't—not now, not without completely losing it.

"Is Jonathan here yet?" Stephanie said instead.

"Yes, and so are most of the guests," Bess added as she peeked out the door. "Oh my gosh! Did you see the flower garlands on the stairway?"

"Soozie made them out of the flower arrangements from yesterday's alumnae luncheon," Holly explained. "Aren't they great?"

Stephanie sighed. The house looked even more beautiful than she'd ever imagined it could be. In front of the living room fireplace, where the ceremony would take place, there were ficus trees decorated with tiny white lights. Dining room chairs were set up in rows, and white ribbons had been looped to form an aisle.

"I'm here," Nancy said, hurrying into the room, looking a little frazzled. "Sorry I'm late. Look. I brought you something blue, Stephanie."

Stephanie took a soft package from Nancy and opened it. Then she reached out and gave her a hug. It was a tiny embroidered handkerchief of the palest blue. "Perfect for crying into," she said.

"And here's something borrowed." Casey came forward with a slim unwrapped box. "So you have to give it back, hon," she joked gently.

Stephanie gasped. Lying on a bed of black satin was a string of lustrous pearls.

"They're real," Casey said casually as she slipped them around Stephanie's neck. "I sensibly bought them with a check from *The President's Daughter.*"

Holly gave her an old book of poems to hold during the ceremony, and Bess gave her a brand-new pen to sign her wedding certificate.

"Now you have something old, something new, something borrowed, and something blue," Bess said.

"The music's starting," Casey called out. "Everyone take your seats. Smile at the groom."

Stephanie felt scared and happy at the same time. "Nancy," she said suddenly, touching Nancy's arm to hold her back. "I just want you to know that this marriage is right. It's not crazy. I'll prove it to you."

Nancy squeezed her hand. "You and Jonathan prove it to yourselves, okay?"

"We're going to have the best marriage in the world."

"So get out there." Nancy grinned.

Stephanie strode down the hall and turned to face the living room, now filled with people. The ribboned aisle seemed very long and scary at first. But when she looked up and saw Jonathan smiling at the end, it suddenly seemed like the most beautiful stroll she could take in her life.

"I, Stephanie Keats, do take thee, Jonathan Baur," Stephanie repeated after the judge. "To have and to hold, for richer or poorer, in sickness and health, till death do us part."

Bess sighed and glanced around the silent room. Tears trickled from the corners of eyes. She herself had had many wedding fantasies in her lifetime. Weddings in quaint country churches. Weddings in austere cathedrals with hundreds of guests. Underwater weddings. Mountaintop weddings.

Still, she thought, she was about a million miles away from actually getting married to someone.

"And do you, Jonathan, take this woman to be your wedded wife . . ."

Instead, Bess's mind was spinning with her favorite lines from *Cat on a Hot Tin Roof.* Jeanne Glasseburg had actually called her into her office to ask her to audition! For the lead!

She squirmed in her seat. If she didn't get going on her lines by tomorrow, she'd blow her audition for sure. Ms. Glasseburg wanted her to read an incredibly huge scene. But she could do it; she knew she could.

"And, therefore, by the power invested in me by the State of Illinois . . ."

Bess shifted in her seat again, looking over her shoulder at the lavish buffet table set up in the dining room. For the first time in a week, she wasn't the least bit hungry. She wasn't thinking about Nancy. And she wasn't thinking about Ned.

I'm thinking about me, she realized. For the first time in a long time, she wasn't thinking about the people she could lean on, but the things she could do to make herself happy.

"I pronounce you husband and wife."

Loud applause startled Bess from her thoughts. She watched as the bride and groom turned to each other and then locked in a passionate kiss that lasted for as long as the ceremony.

An hour later the wedding party was in full swing. The Kappas had a legendary collection of old big-band recordings. Nancy was doing the jitterbug with Casey. Bess was dancing with Stephanie's bouquet. And George was wandering around, listening in on conversations—feeling lost.

"I hear that the bride and groom are making out in the Kappas' secret ritual room," she heard someone whisper in her ear.

George turned around. "Will!" she exclaimed.

"Quiet. I won't tell," he joked.

A happy warmth went through George at the sight of Will. He was just standing there in his jeans, casually nibbling grapes from the buffet and acting as if he crashed wedding parties every day of his life. As angry as she had been feeling toward him, she was thrilled to see him.

"So did all of the wedding vows go okay?" he asked. "I mean, did Stephanie decide to break up with Jonathan just before the ceremony? Or did she slip party ice down the judge's back?"

George giggled. "Stephanie was actually very well-behaved," she told him.

"How boring," Will said. Suddenly, he grabbed George's hand, gave her her coat, and pulled her toward the door outside. "I won't bite. I just want to talk."

George followed, mentally rehearsing what she would say. She had decided that for now she wasn't ready for sex with Will—no matter how much she loved him. If he had trouble hearing that again, then too bad.

But to her surprise, Will's attitude was completely different.

"I'm sorry," he said right off. "I'm sorry about everything."

George stood there, stunned. She looked into his dark eyes and saw that he was serious. "I was acting like a jerk," he went on as they walked outside.

George grinned. "I couldn't agree more."

"I just . . ." Will searched for the words to make his point. "Stephanie's wedding has made me think a lot. I mean, she can't suddenly declare herself an adult just by getting married."

George nodded, letting him continue.

"You can't just say, 'Okay, I'm an adult now.' It takes time to grow up. And there are lots of things I'm not ready to handle."

"Like what?" George wanted to know. They went around to the back of the Kappa house and dropped down on an old patio bench to talk.

"Where do I start?" Will went on. "I'm not ready for marriage, children, mortgages, exercise programs, or sensible cars."

George laughed. "Good."

"But this is what I'm trying to say," Will said, turning to George. "I know you're not ready for sex. You can't handle it right now. I understand. It's not easy, but I'd hate it if you lied to me about that. Especially about that."

George put her hands around his neck. "You know, when I first got to that Sekhmet Society meeting, all I could think was that most of these women have never experienced a healthy relationship. They were pretty angry, Will. They don't know what it's like to stay true to yourself when you're involved with a guy. Not like I know," she added softly. "I'm lucky to have a guy who can handle it."

"I love you, George," Will whispered. "I've been acting like a spoiled kid, and I'm sorry."

George stood up with Will and kissed him tenderly.

"Let's just be together," Will said gently. "We can kiss. We can cuddle. We can just be together. But let's not drop everything."

"Kissing and cuddling, huh?" George asked.

"Yeah."

George moved in for another kiss. "I can get into that."

"Please come in, Miss Drew," Wilder University's athletic director, Carl Jackson, was saying.

Nancy had been waiting outside his office. Stephanie's wedding party had just begun when Judd's call came through at the Kappa house.

"I'm at the athletic center," Judd had said in a rush of words. "You've got to get down here to Carl Jackson's office. It's really important."

As Carl Jackson ushered her into his large trophy-lined office, Nancy halted abruptly. There, sitting on chairs and leaning against sideboards and window frames, was Judd and nearly every member of the Wilder University men's cross-country team, with the exception of its team captain, Rudy Milton.

"Hi, Nancy," Judd said, walking up to her. "We've told Mr. Jackson everything."

"Good for you, Judd," she said, resting a hand on his arm.

"We wanted you here, Nancy," Mr. Jackson spoke up.

"I won't tolerate secrecy in this department, especially when it concerns the welfare of our athletes," the director went on. "The men here have told me about Coach Hayes's use of caffeine supplements before meets. They came here together, willing to risk their reputations and their scholarships, because they saw something wrong and they wanted to correct it."

There was a knock at the director's office door and everyone suddenly turned to look.

"Hey, Carl," Nancy heard Coach Hayes's cheerful greeting. "What's up? What did you—"

Nancy watched as Coach Hayes's eyes scanned the solemn faces in the room. His face suddenly filled with panic.

"Hey, fellows," he said in a weak voice.

"Sit down, Chuck," the director said.

Wordlessly, Coach Hayes obeyed.

"The men here say that you have encouraged—even coerced—them into taking high doses of caffeine prior to competition," the director said. "In fact, they tell me that Rick Alexander took these pills to overcome the symptoms of a virus he'd contracted—so that he could still compete. And you allowed it."

Coach Hayes looked around the room, his face suddenly filled with contempt. "So," he snarled, "this is what it comes down to, huh? You guys just aren't willing to do what it takes, are you?"

"Chuck—" the director began.

"You don't deserve to win," the coach shouted. "You want to make up some crazy story about drugs and ruin me, do you?"

"It's the truth," Judd stated. "You should have told Rick to lay off the stuff. Instead you encouraged him."

"Shut up, Wright," the coach snapped.

"I've talked with our legal department, Chuck," the director said. "And we're prepared to charge you in court with reckless endangerment of our athletes' lives."

The coach started to bolt, but two uniformed officers were waiting in the hall.

"I called them in," the director explained sadly. "Just in case you tried to run, Chuck."

Nancy let out a long sigh as the coach was led away. It was over. She was glad to see the coach finally get stopped, but she couldn't help feeling an undercurrent of sadness, too. Coach Hayes must have been so desperate to win, she thought. Didn't he realize that winning wasn't worth the price of his career—or the price of his athletes' lives? A few minutes later the crowd in the room began to break up and Nancy felt Judd step beside her.

"Thanks," he said quietly. "I don't know what would have happened if you hadn't gotten involved."

Nancy nodded as she looked into his eyes. "I'm glad I did get involved," she whispered. "I . . ."

Suddenly they both realized that the room was empty. Without finishing her sentence, Nancy leaned toward him and felt Judd's lips on hers. The office faded away. And everything in her life felt as if it were starting all over again.

"Where are you taking me?" Stephanie asked, slipping closer to Jonathan on the front seat. It was late, and Stephanie was still wearing the white gown she'd been married in. A slim band of gold was shining on the ring finger of her left hand.

"It's a secret," Jonathan replied, smiling as he headed out of town on the highway.

Stephanie felt so happy she didn't know if she could take any more perfection. Everything about her wedding had come off like a dream.

"I know!" Stephanie exclaimed as Jonathan slowed and turned right onto a long gravel road leading through trees up a slope. "You're taking me to the Benborough Inn."

"You're right," Jonathan said, sounding a little disappointed that she'd guessed their honeymoon site.

"Oh." Stephanie clapped her hands together. "Wonderful! I've always wanted to stay there. It's supposed to be so romantic."

Jonathan pulled up to the sprawling, three-story, restored farmhouse all lit up, as if it were waiting just for them.

"Welcome," the woman at the reception desk said warmly. "And congratulations. We have your room all ready for you."

Stephanie melted when she saw their honeymoon suite. It was roomy, with a fireplace in front of the double bed, a homemade quilt, and a romantic balcony overlooking the gardens.

"Come on, Mrs. Baur," Jonathan murmured. "This is where I get to carry you over the threshold, remember?"

Stephanie giggled as he swept her inside and shut the door. A moment later he popped open a bottle of champagne and held up two glasses.

"I love you, Stephanie," Jonathan said tenderly, tipping his glass to hers.

Stephanie sipped the champagne, then set down her glass and kissed her husband. She flashed on all of the movies she'd seen about weddings and honeymoons. They were all so different from what today had been. And yet today had been absolutely perfect.

Now that the vows had been spoken and the wedding cake had been eaten, there wasn't a dreamy fade-out like in the movies. There wasn't the fizzy rush or roller-coaster ride that Stephanie had imagined. Instead there was only the sense that what was happening was very real, and so was the man opposite her. It was real and Jonathan was real.

Stephanie felt something deep and quiet form inside.

Maybe it's happiness, she thought. Or maybe it was peace. Or maybe it was just the feeling that she'd found a way to be. A place she could come home to. And best of all a person who actually loved her.

NEXT IN NANCY DREW ON CAMPUS™:

After his breakup with Nancy, Jake swore no more dating, no more women, no more romance. But when beautiful Russian transfer student Nadia Karloff enters the picture, Jake decides to make an exception. There's just one catch: Dating Nadia means dealing with Nadia's suitemate—Nancy Drew! But Nancy's got problems of her own. Is her father going to spend *all* of his time with his new girlfriend? And what happened to photographer Gary Friedman? Did he fall or was he pushed to his death? Working on the story for the *Wilder Times,* Nancy will also have to work things out with—who else?—Jake . . . in *In and Out of Love,* Nancy Drew on Campus #22.

R·L·STINE'S GHOSTS OF FEAR STREET®

1	Hide and Shriek	52941-2/$3.99
2	Who's Been Sleeping in My Grave?	52942-0/$3.99
3	Attack of the Aqua Apes	52943-9/$3.99
4	Nightmare in 3-D	52944-7/$3.99
5	Stay Away From the Tree House	52945-5/$3.99
6	Eye of the Fortuneteller	52946-3/$3.99
7	Fright Knight	52947-1/$3.99
8	The Ooze	52948-X/$3.99
9	Revenge of the Shadow People	52949-8/$3.99
10	The Bugman Lives	52950-1/$3.99
11	The Boy Who Ate Fear Street	00183-3/$3.99
12	Night of the Werecat	00184-1/$3.99
13	How to be a Vampire	00185-X/$3.99
14	Body Switchers from Outer Space	00186-8/$3.99
15	Fright Christmas	00187-6/$3.99
16	Don't Ever get Sick at Granny's	00188-4/$3.99
17	House of a Thousand Screams	00190-6/$3.99
18	Camp Fear Ghouls	00191-4/$3.99
19	Three Evil Wishes	00189-2/$3.99
20	Spell of the Screaming Jokers	00192-2/$3.99

Christopher Pike presents....
a frighteningly fun new series for your younger brothers and sisters!

1 The Secret Path 53725-3/$3.50
2 The Howling Ghost 53726-1/$3.50
3 The Haunted Cave 53727-X/$3.50
4 Aliens in the Sky 53728-8/$3.99
5 The Cold People 55064-0/$3.99
6 The Witch's Revenge 55065-9/$3.99
7 The Dark Corner 55066-7/$3.99
8 The Little People 55067-5/$3.99
9 The Wishing Stone 55068-3/$3.99
10 The Wicked Cat 55069-1/$3.99
11 The Deadly Past 55072-1/$3.99
12 The Hidden Beast 55073-X/$3.99
13 The Creature in the Teacher 00261-9/$3.99
14 The Evil House 00262-7/$3.99
15 Invasion of the No-Ones 00263-5/$3.99
16 Time Terror 00264-3/$3.99

A MINSTREL® BOOK